Raven

By

Tara Moeller

DreamPunk Press

DreamPunk Press

This is a work of fiction.
Names, characters, businesses, places, events or incidents are either the products of the author's imagination or used in a fictitious manner. Any resemblance to actual person, living or dead, or actual events is purely coincidental.

RAVEN

Published by DreamPunk Press, Norfolk, VA

www.dreampunkpress.com

dreamer-in-chief@dreampunkpress.com

Cover art: ©

Cover design by: Tara Moeller

OpenDyslexic font from www.opendyslexic.org

First Edition

ISBN 13: 978-1-954214-11-8 (Open Dyslexic)

ISBN 13: 978-1-954214-12-5 (Deja Vu)

ISBN 13: 978-1-954214-13-2 (ePub)

Printed in the USA

One for sorrow
Two for mirth
Three for a wedding
Four for a birth
Five for silver
Six for Gold
Seven for a Secret
never to be told
Eight for a wish
Nine for a kiss
Ten for a bird
you should never miss
Eleven for Health
Twelve for Wealth
Thirteen for the very
devil himself.

One
A Beautiful Saturday Morning

5 June 2021

The sun was bright, the sky a pure, cloudless blue. There was a breeze, cooling the heat on my skin where I sat on my balcony, staring at the mountains, sipping my first cup of coffee.

Being isolated on my small balcony, I wasn't worried about wearing a mask or social distancing. No one else was even up at this hour.

I'd slept in after a long Friday at work, finishing a report that just had to be done ASAP. The Head of the Finance Department always needed reports by Monday, even when they only asked for it on Friday morning. There had been a reprieve during the early days of the pandemic lockdown, but now, everything was pretty much back to normal, near-impossible expectations.

No matter we were still in the midst of a pandemic.

Since I was single and not dating, and my boss had three kids—one of them a toddler—I had no real issue staying late on Fridays, especially as she was really good at making sure I was compensated for the extra time.

Of course, it could always be done on Saturday, and on the few occasions when I had Friday-night plans, I would do that. But honestly, I preferred just staying late on Friday and having the whole weekend still for myself.

Saturday morning coffee on my balcony, in my tiny condo, was a treat I didn't like giving up. I usually followed it with a quick walk to my favorite café for brunch, sometimes with a friend, but usually not.

I didn't have that many friends. I'd never been good at making them, except for Raven. She and I had been friends since kindergarten, maybe even earlier.

This particular Saturday, I was never so fortunate—or unfortunate—that I'd stayed late.

My phone trilled on the little glass table-top beside me; it was my mother. She usually called on Sundays, but a Saturday call wasn't out of the ordinary, especially if there was something going on at church that could take the whole day.

"Good morning!" And it was.

There was a pause on the line, then a hiccupped sob and a soggy sniffle.

"Mom?"

Oh, God, had something happened to Dad?

A heavy sigh. "Hello, Anna."

Then nothing.

I swallowed and cleared my throat. "What's wrong?"

She heaved an even longer sigh; I could almost feel it. "Hank called your Dad this morning. Early."

Oh. Okay. Though it didn't explain why Mom sounded like she was crying, my tension eased and I settled back in my chair. I'd sat up at that first muffled sound of sorrow.

"I'm sorry, honey. Hank said...he told your Dad..." there was a loud sob, "Raven's dead."

Raven was dead? What? When? How? Had...

I reminded myself to breathe. It came out raggedy and harsh.

"Anna?" Mom's voice sounded far away.

The sun still gleamed, its heat intense on my face; the blue of the sky deepened, seeming to seep into me, invading the pleasure of a Saturday of nothing to do.

Raven was gone.

We'd been friends forever—literally. Our families had lived next door to each other in military housing before we'd been born, our mothers happy to have someone so close in similar circumstances. They'd become fast friends.

And, when they'd both given birth to their first children, we had become fast friends, too. Though I don't remember much of that before kindergarten.

Raven was only a week older than me; though technically, I should have been older. She'd decided to arrive early—three whole weeks early—surprising everyone, especially her parents.

My parents had been the ones to take her mother to the hospital. Her father had been on duty, and had had to wait for his relief to arrive before he could leave.

But then, Raven had always been impatient.

"Thanks for calling me, Mom." The words were half-choked, my throat having difficulty forming the words around the lump clogging it. Swallowing didn't help. It was there to stay until I had a chance to cry.

"It was so sudden." Mom's voice was sodden in the speaker part of my cell. "I don't know exactly what happened; Hank called Jim this morning early to let us know. I thought...I thought everything was good now. She'd left Norfolk, you know."

I reminded myself that Mom didn't know that whole story. Nor did Dad or even Hank, really.

Hank was Raven's father; Jim was mine.

None of them knew the full truth of anything that had gone down last summer. And I wasn't going to tell them now.

"Okay." My voice still didn't want to work right.

"Dad left right after the call. I guess Hank sounded like he needed someone. I haven't heard from Gayle yet. I'm not sure it's my place to call her, just in case no one else has gotten hold of her, you know?"

Gayle and Hank hadn't stayed married. The Navy, and the constant moving—after having been in Norfolk for a couple of rotations—and uncertainty of place, had taken its toll on their relationship, and they'd parted ways when Raven was in middle school.

And that breakup had made an even bigger demands on Raven's relationship with her parents. She's been pulled at by each, a prize to be won, an award for whichever parent could better the other.

Although, I suppose, their relationship—or the volatility of it—had been the toll-taker, and the price, in the end, had been steep. Their breakup had been more of a relief than anything else.

Gayle liked to tell the story of how Raven had gone through a Goth phase starting in sixth grade. She liked to blame Hank for that and his lack of "being around" for his daughter.

That's when my friend had chosen the name "Raven." Up until then, she'd been Kelly. But in sixth grade, she'd become Raven, not answering to any other name but that.

I suppose the name suited her, with her long, blue-black hair that hung straight no matter how hot the curling iron, and the long, straight, tapered nose and jutting chin. There was a sharpness about her features that the name Kelly just didn't suit.

And she'd always liked dark things. Black was her favorite color, and she'd taken to wearing black nail polish in fourth grade. She'd loved the R.L. Stine books, and had quickly graduated to V.C. Andrews, Stephen King, and Edgar Allen Poe.

We'd sneak in watching horror movies on our sleepovers, me huddled under the blanket, eyes only cracked open, snuggled up against her warmth.

But middle school was not about being dark or her dad's absence.

Middle school—and the Goth phase her mother loves to lament about—had been all about Archie McMichael. He was a seventh grader, who also loved everything dark—stuff even darker than what Raven liked—and she had fallen in hard crush with him.

He had been the ultimate middle-school bad boy, sneaking cigarettes, alcohol, and glances down girls' shirts. He also liked to cut himself, and would show off the scars on his forearms to anyone who would look at them.

When she was eighteen, she'd made the name change legal, even taking "Poe" as a middle name.

I think that was specifically to piss off her mother. Until then, her middle name had been Gayle, after her mother.

I'm not saying her mother didn't love her...just that they really didn't get along and never understood each other.

She'd spent many a summer at the same camp as me, Gayle arranging things with my mother so that we could still maintain our friendship. Her father had been onboard with that plan; his career took him all over the globe, and he hadn't been physically present for much of her teen-hood, and she'd lived with her mother.

We'd been as close as sisters, maybe closer. I had a sister, Gemma, but she'd been a free-spirit sort and I'd already had Raven by the time she came along. I might have even resented her, being a four-year-old when she was born.

There had never been any rivalry between me and Raven—not even about those middle-school boys. I'd always been on her side and she'd always been on mine.

I took a shaky breath. "Call me when you know more, okay?" I needed to get off the call. My eyes burned with hot tears and I thought I might throw up around that lump. It tasted like bile.

"I will." Sniffing, Mom hung up.

I stared out from the balcony, at the horizon of dusty mesa and scrub. Someone blared a horn; the rest of the world was getting up and going out, starting their Saturday by taking their kids to practice or the park, or heading out for their own activities. I'd heard the new yoga studio was a big hit, even though classes were only half the number of participants and everyone had to be vaccinated and wear masks.

Colorado Springs was a retirement town; a lot of folks moved west where the dry air was good for their joints. I'd taken advantage of that and taken a job in health care management at Memorial Hospital. It was a pretty easy job, in reality. Young folks are pretty healthy and most of the retirees that could afford to move here had good health insurance.

I ran health care and budget reports. Lots of reports. Most were automated, so it wasn't really what I thought of as work, more just monitoring the system to make sure it output something legible at the end.

The pandemic, and everything else this past year, had been rough, but that was mostly over now. We knew what to do—mask up and socially distance, get vaccinated and boosted, and work from home and order our groceries for pickup. We had a new normal and most of us were adjusting.

At least, I was. Since I worked in management—monitoring all those reports—it was easy for me to remain at home, log into the system, and work from my laptop.

And now, just as life was finally returning to a semblance of routine, Raven was gone.

My life would never be normal again.

Two
I Should Have Known

January 2020

When I saw Raven before the pandemic hit its first sustained surge. We'd both planned to go home for Christmas to be with our respective families and then meet up for the New Year in New York.

I'd seen my parents in Illinois—my father was now a contracted instructor at the Naval Training Center electronics school—and she'd spent a week with her father at his duty station in San Diego—he was a Command Master Chief in his last tour before retiring. In six months, he was due to be out and starting as an instructor, too, although not electronics.

New York hadn't worked out, as it was just too expensive for either of us after our respective family trips, but we'd been able to make Charleston, South Carolina work. We didn't get to see snow together, but we'd had much nicer weather than what we would have had in New York. We'd also gotten into a party at a historic hotel in big floppy-brimmed hats while drinking mint juleps. And walk on the beach after, in bare feet.

We'd gotten a few stares, but why would we care? We were on vacation.

Raven needed cheering up. Her boyfriend of two years had dumped her for a job in Seattle. There was no way she could move right away; she'd been finishing up the last course for her hospitality management degree at community college. She didn't have the funds or the job to move out on her own, so she was sleeping on the sofa of a classmate.

He'd been a jerk anyway. He'd looked down at her attending a two-year school.

I think she'd known it was ending, and he'd known it, and had used the move as a way to force the breakup before they had to get serious. She was still sad, though; she'd told me she'd felt a bit like a failure, because he'd been her longest-running relationship and her dad had liked him.

But it didn't take much to cheer her up; all I'd had to do was mention that maybe we could plan a cruise to take together.

"Where would we go?" Raven was ankle deep in the Atlantic Ocean, her black jeans rolled up to her knees, her black t-shirt fitted to her form.

Shrugging, I threw out a couple of ideas. I was dressed similarly—although I wore blue jeans and a pink tee—"The Caribbean? The Aegean?" I snickered. "Alaska?"

"Alaska?" Raven splashed water at me, using her foot as a scoop.

I dodged and laughed.

"There's SNOW in Alaska." Raven rolled her eyes, but a smile played over her lips.

"Okay," I swiped at the water on my legs, "so the Caribbean or Aegean?"

"We'd have to fly to Rome or something for the Aegean, yeah?" Raven looked out at the horizon. There was a ketch passing, its double mast slicing up into the deepening sky.

I sighed. "Yeah." It would be nice to see Italy again; following my dad's path, I'd signed up for the Navy and been stationed there for two years, in Gaeta. I hadn't made the Navy a career though, and taken courses while in, finishing up my Bachelors within a year after my four-year stint.

We weren't made of money so...

"So, Caribbean?"

"Works for me." I jostled her in the side. "You okay with that?"

Raven placed a finger on her chin and moued her lips, cocking out one hip in a jaunty pose. "I guess." Then she giggled and dashed from the water and across the sand of the beach. "Last one to the boardwalk buys the drinks!"

I let her win; that's my story, even though she got there a full half a minute before I did. Turning back to the beach, I leaned against the short wall along the boardwalk, taking in deep breaths. "No fair."

"Of course not." Raven was already breathing normally, but didn't say anything about how hard it was for me to catch mine.

I'd been living in Colorado for a couple of years already, so the air seemed so thick on the east coast now. I could almost feel the moisture from it pooling in my lungs. I'd have never thought this ex-Sailor wouldn't like being near the ocean.

Raven waited beside me, humming. Then, "One week or two?"

"Huh?"

"The cruise? One week or two?"

I sniffed. "Probably depends on how much they cost."

"I suppose." She was quiet a moment. "When do we want to do it?"

"End of summer?" I was breathing easier now, so we started along the boardwalk towards our hotel.

Raven frowned. "Not sure I can save up enough in six months."

"Okay. Next summer?"

"That'll be your 10-year high school reunion."

"Even better." I snickered.

Laughing, Raven almost tripped over a crooked plank. "Yeah. I don't want to go to mine, either. Even if it's the following year. Maybe this can become a regular thing for us."

We hadn't finished high school together, and not just because Raven had failed the year her parents had finalized their divorced when she was in the ninth grade. We hadn't attended any of high school together; I had moved with my Navy family.

And Raven had shifted between living with her mother and then her father, when he was stationed in the states.

That we were still friends, after all this time, may have been an anomaly, but we'd still done so much together.

First summer of away-camp together, followed by another three years of summer camps together.

Got drunk for the first time together when I'd turned 21—Raven hadn't waited for her first legal drink, but she'd been careful to only drink one.

We'd also joined the Navy together. Well, at the same time anyways.

Though we'd been on opposite coasts when enlisting— I waited a year for Raven to graduate so I'd finished a few classes at community college—we'd managed to get stationed in Norfolk together, undesignated on the USS JOHN C STENNIS. She'd wound up with galley duty and fell in love with it and I'd struck for electronics tech, to follow in my dad's footsteps, but electrical current didn't agree with me (shocking!), and I got sent to Corpsman school instead. I think that I was a legacy enlistment helped.

"We can celebrate on the cruise. Just the two of us." I suggested. "It can be our own reunion—of a sort."

Holding hands, we skipped along the boardwalk. Folks stared at us, but I didn't care. Friends can hold hands; it didn't mean anything.

Of course, some old biddy said something to another old biddy—it was okay that they were on vacay together, I guess?—and Raven got embarrassed and dropped my hand. It was ridiculous; it didn't mean anything.

We weren't a couple. Just friends.

I'd never really liked dating, even after having a really nice boyfriend in high school. We'd done prom and everything, but it just wasn't me.

It was Raven, though. She been dating since the end of middle school (although not

Archie McMichael); I'd gotten to hear all about Kyle, a high school sophomore, three years older than her, who'd taken her out for a movie and kiss. She'd told the story every other day at our last summer camp together. By the end, I could tell the story all by myself, in several versions.

I never liked that story.

Or the one about Seth, whom she'd dated casually in high school, or Robert who had taken her for prom and she'd had graduation sex with.

I'd never thought any of them were good enough for her.

That night after dinner, I went up to our room while she stayed down to listen to the piano player and finish her last drink. The room was full of people, and I figured she was safe.

I fell asleep before she came up; never even heard her come in. But the morning confirmed my suspicion that I hadn't had to worry. I got to hear all about what had happened over breakfast.

She'd met someone. His name was Brett or something like that. She told me all about him while I ate my toast and jam and coffee with cream and sugar.

Raven didn't eat; she never did when she was excited.

And she was so excited that she'd met him. He was cute. He was funny. And he lived in Norfolk, the same as her, although in a different part.

"Brent said he's a teacher, but I don't know of what."

Okay, his name was *Brent*. I didn't like that name. It sounded like the name of someone who'd be stuffy and stuck up. I told myself if he was, she'd dump him soon enough.

And I'd get to cheer her up again.

I couldn't wait to meet him. See for myself what I thought of him, in person.

But I didn't get to meet him; he left that morning while we were eating.

Part of me was glad of their meeting and her excitement about it. She was smiling again, confident again, in love with life again—though I hoped not with this Brent fellow, at least not yet. There was a lot of time for him to turn out to be a waste-of-time low-life.

For all I knew, he didn't even live in Norfolk and had only said that to try to make an easy hook up. I refused to think about what time Raven might have come back to our room.

"What do you want to do today?" Raven's enthusiasm for the day was catching.

"Browse the downtown and do a little shopping?" I always got my parents something when I traveled; Dad had always gotten something for me and Mom when he was away. It was almost a tradition. We only had a couple days left in Charleston, and I had nothing for them yet.

Raven cocked her head, staring off a bit out the window. It was breezy and a little clouded over. Not a great day for the beach.

"Sounds like a plan." She frowned at the clouds. "Though we might want check the weather and ask for a couple of umbrellas. It looks a bit like rain."

By the time we made it out of the hotel and purchased a couple of retractable umbrellas from the gift shop across the street, it was drizzling. But it was still relatively warm, and we had on sweaters, jeans, and rain jackets, so we were good to go.

Raven was bubbly all day, and even got a phone call from Brent midafternoon. He wanted her to know he was safely in Norfolk, and that he hoped to take her to dinner when she got in. He could even pick her up from the airport if she needed a ride.

My friend was a smart girl, and said no to the pick-up, but yes to dinner. Brent didn't seem to make any fuss with her about the first no, so my estimate of him ticked up a bit.

Maybe he wasn't so bad after all. At least he seemed to be making Raven happy.

Three
It Only Got Worse

April 2020

"Hey, Anna."

"Hey, Raven. How are you?" She sounded fine; not sick or anything. Relieved, I put the call on speaker.

I was in my car, driving home from work with my laptop and a few reports I couldn't run out and print from home. There weren't many, and I only had to go into work about once a month, fully double-masked and drenching my hands and anything I touched with sanitizer. Other than that, the pandemic just meant I was doing most of my work from my bedroom.

For the nurses and doctors at the hospital, it was a different story. Long, hard shifts, patients who were deathly sick—dying—with little they could do to help. I'd reminded my boss that I'd been a Corpsman in the Navy, if they needed volunteers, but she told me to keep hush and run my reports.

"I'm fine. My job...not so much." Her voice got low over the phone.

"Oh?" I checked the time and pulled into the parking lot of the Safeway near my house. I had to pick up my grocery order, but it wouldn't be ready for another 15 minutes. My commute to work and home was getting shorter as more and more folks were either working from home or laid off and regular events were cancelled.

There was a deep, gusty sigh. "The restaurant is closing and I've been laid off."

"Oh, I'm sorry." I wished it was an April Fools' joke a day late, but I knew it wasn't. The world was different, parts of it falling apart. I was still working, albeit from home, my paycheck unaffected by the closures and mask mandates. Even though I worked at a hospital, administrative staff weren't expected to come into the office unless absolutely necessary.

"Yeah. It sucks, but I'm going to move in with Brent." Raven's voice grew faint for a moment, like she'd moved away from her phone, then it got clear and loud again. "He's going to be working from home, and if I move in with him, I won't have to worry about paying rent, just my car insurance and cell phone."

"Are you sure that's a good idea?" I still hadn't met her new boyfriend yet, hadn't heard anything about him from her dad via my dad. Now that Hank was in Illinois, the two were back to being best buds—although, at a distance. All I knew was that Raven and Brent had started dating soon after she'd gotten home from our vacation in Charleston.

"What else can I do? I don't have a job anymore."

Her four years working in a Navy mess, taking a couple of nutrition courses on ship, then finishing with a two-year Associates in Hospitality Management, had transitioned to managing an upscale fast-food restaurant as a civilian. Though it wasn't her dream job, she was good at it and it used her training. From what I could tell, she was moving up, too. She'd become the manager only a year ago, getting the promotion over another assistant manager that had been there for years.

"What about staying with your dad?"

"My mom would never speak to me again. You know how that goes."

Yeah. That divorce had been long and nasty. Still wasn't pretty.

I thought about my small condo—the one bedroom where I had set up a desk in the corner for work and the single bathroom—

and the fold-out sofa that needed a new mattress.

"Do you want to come stay with me?"

Raven barked out a laugh. "Girl, I've seen photos of your place. It's not big enough for you. That place looks smaller than berthing on the STENNIS."

She wasn't wrong. When we'd been stationed on the carrier, we might have had a small area for sleeping, but there'd been a gym and recreation areas. There was always space if you knew where to look for it.

"Okay. So, moving in with Brent is your only option?"

"It's probably not my only option, but it's the one I think I can take. If I hadn't spent my savings on our trip—and that isn't to make you feel guilty!—I could manage the three months or so that I'll be out of work. I can stay with my boyfriend that long."

Three months...

I thought about the data I'd seen about the virus. The numbers I'd been asked to crunch for the hospital. The preparations some of the doctors thought we should take but upper management scoffed at.

"What if it's longer than three months? What if this thing is a lot more dangerous than folks think?"

"Well then...staying with Brent is definitely the right choice. No way I could stand my dad for more than three months!" Raven's laughter filled my car.

It was infectious and I just had to laugh with her. "Point."

I put my car in drive and maneuvered to the grocery pick-up lane. I had the printout from when I'd ordered last night in my purse and dug it out from the bottom.

"What is that noise?"

"I'm in my car. Picking up groceries. Hold on." I put my mask on and rolled down my door window to tap the button that would let me talk to the employee that would bring out my order.

Once I'd gotten confirmation that they'd be right out and to make sure my trunk was open, I punched the open-trunk button and watched the small hatch rise behind me.

"Okay." I let Raven know I was listening again. "Did you bring it up or Brent?"

There was a pause. "Um...I think he offered. We were talking after I was laid off and mentioned that I wasn't sure about paying my bills, and he said I could always stay with someone. We were talking a bit more and then he said I could stay with him."

"Is he ready if this thing lasts for a while?"

"He gets to work from home. Plan is, classes will be done via Zoom."

"That's not what I mean." I watched a person in a bright orange safety vest set paper bags in my trunk, close the trunk lid, and give me a thumbs up. I couldn't see their face; it was covered by a black mask and a bright yellow bandana.

I smiled and waved and put my car in drive. Taking my mask off, I wound the ear ties around my gear shift to keep it from falling on the floor.

"I mean…" What did I mean? "Like…how many bedrooms does his place have? Does he have a home office? An extra bathroom in case one of you do get sick?"

"You should have gone into nursing instead of hospital management."

I could just imagine my friend rolling her eyes at me. "Come on, Raven. How big is his place?"

She was silent for a long moment.

I stopped for a family of five heading into the grocery store—both adults wore masks but not their three kids—waving and smiling, but my smile was fake. Those kids were old enough to understand and wear a mask.

"Brent is a teacher."

"Uh-huh. So you said before." I made the right turn onto the main drag and sped up. "Do you know what he teaches yet?"

"He teaches at Old Dominion University. A tenured professor. Of religion."

I almost slammed on the brakes. "How old is Brent?"

"I mean, he's not OLD. Just...older."

"Raven..."

"He doesn't look it, though. He looks younger...and fit, if you know what I mean." She snickered. "Anyways. He has a nice house; three bedrooms, two baths, a home office, a HUGE gourmet kitchen-"

I giggled. "You should have just become a chef." I wondered—briefly—if she liked Brent for himself or for his kitchen.

"Maybe...but he's got lots of room. I would have my own bedroom and bathroom."

Like I thought that scenario was likely. After all, he looked younger and was fit.

Raven was gorgeous. Even without makeup, she had a natural glow to her skin. And her eyes were a stand-out blue, clear and deep and piercing; if she stared directly at you, your stomach would curl and knot up because you'd feel she was staring right into your soul.

"If you just need help with your rent, I have savings I could dip into." I made more money than Raven and had no issues sharing.

I'd used my GI benefits to finish my Bachelor's in Health Care Management, so I hadn't needed to dip into any savings for school, even though that's what I'd initially put it away for.

"Dad already made that offer. I can't say yes to you after saying no to him."

"And your mom?" I wasn't sure I wanted to know what Gayle thought.

"She thinks moving in with Brent is a good idea. It will give me an idea if this is the real thing or not." Raven snorted. "She even suggested that we could have an online wedding and save a bundle."

I groaned. "What if it isn't? And we're still in a pandemic with everything closed up? Where do you go?"

"I either go stay with my dad or camp out on your sofa."

Four
Worries Multiplied

June 2020

"So-"

Raven had called. We were on the phone and I was streaming Good Omens on Prime for the third time, the sound muted since we were talking.

"-there won't be a wedding anytime soon."

"Oh?" I tried not to sound happier than I should be at the prospect and covered myself by dipping a homemade French fry into a mix of mayo and ketchup and a dash of sriracha and crunching down on it. It was Friday night; no way to go out with the lockdowns, so I made things special as best I could. "I didn't think it was really in the cards."

So far, I'd gained ten pounds. And learned how to make ice cream and fudge. The fries were made in a new air fryer, an attempt to combat the ten pounds.

I might have done some pandemic boredom shopping.

"Yeah."

What sounded like the wail of a baby erupted in the background on the line. "What are you watching?" Raven usually muted the TV when we were on the phone.

"Nothing." Raven sighed, but it ended in a groan. "That is Twila; Brent's other girlfriend's new baby."

Other girlfriend? I straightened up from my slouch on my sofa, pausing the feed to my TV so I wasn't distracted by Michael Sheen's cherubic grin. "Do tell."

"Twila's mother, Stella, is one of his undergraduate students. She showed up with the baby two days ago. Brent explained to me this morning that she has nowhere else to go, so he's letting her stay here in one of the other guest rooms. I think it has more to do with keeping her quiet, so he doesn't lose his job, though I'm sure that's why she came here."

The wail in the background got sharper.

The moan from Raven was muffled. "That kid never shuts up." Her whisper was harsh.

"I'm sorry." I thought a moment "Do you want to come here?" I scanned the room, wondering how to make room for her. I'd do it if I had to.

"How?" Raven sounded like she was ready to cry. "Travel is restricted. I can't get on a plane, even if I could get the money together for a ticket."

The pandemic was really making a mess of people's lives, though, in my opinion, it would be much better if we'd taken better action in the beginning, or even now.

I took in a long breath. Airplanes were out, and so were trains and buses. Anything close to mass transit was shut down due to the easy spread of COVID. Could I drive to Norfolk to bring Raven back? I couldn't drive straight there; I would need to stop overnight at least once.

Would staying overnight at a hotel be safe, considering the virus and I wouldn't really know that the room had been cleaned? I suppose I could take bleach with me. And gloves and extra masks. I could grab some from work.

Hell, would I even be able to find a hotel or motel that was open? Were they allowed to be open?

A quick internet search showed it all depended on the state, and there were several different sets of rules between here and Virginia.

Fuck. Why was this so hard?

"Anna? Are you still there?"

Startled, I almost dropped my cell phone. I'd forgotten I was still talking with Raven. "Yes, I'm here. Sorry. I was trying to figure out a way to get you out of there."

Raven's laugh was short and high-pitched. "Anna, don't worry. I'm just over-reacting. I'll be fine here. I have my own room and bathroom, and everyone else...well, they have their own space, too."

The background noise quietened a little.

"See?" Raven tried to laugh again. "Stella's being a good mother and tending to the baby."

But I wasn't sure. What if another student-girlfriend showed up with a baby? Was there room for more?

"Hey, Anna. I'm going to go. Catch a nap while I can. I'll call you in a couple days."

"Okay. Take care. Call me sooner if you need me."

I love you.

Five
Getting Involved

July 2020

The silver bars on the Navy Lieutenant's shoulder winked in the glare from the light they were using to illuminate their face for the Zoom meeting. She wasn't wearing a cover, since she was inside, at her desk, but her hair was in a messy bun that looked a millimeter away from falling out completely. Her eyes were blood-shot and dark-rimmed, and her face was pale.

She looked exhausted.

This wasn't the usual peppy, reserve-unit leader I was used to.

She sounded exhausted, too. "I'm sorry to call this meeting on short notice like this, but the Commander needs volunteers to call up for service."

We were on Zoom, having gotten a brief text notice last night after 10 pm to check our email inboxes. The email was also brief, simply stating that there would be a unit Zoom call at 0800 in the morning with a link to connect.

I'd been one of the first to call in and wait.

Lieutenant Hennessy had gotten on at 0759, waiting only a few seconds before starting the meeting.

"This shouldn't be unexpected. The situation all over the country is dire. We've been asked to activate as many reservists as possible to help." She sighed and rubbed her eyes with ink-stained fingers. "I'm not sure how much help we'll be, but there it is."

I hit the little button to raise my hand.

"Yes, Johnson."

"I'm a Corpsman. I have no issue volunteering."

The Lieutenant shuffled papers on her desk, the crumpling overpowering her mic for a moment. "You willing to head to Portsmouth Naval?"

"Yes, ma'am."

She wrote something on a paper. "I'll send you your orders via email. You'll probably be flying out from Peterson, but the email will have specifics. Right now, the plan is to activate you for a month, but it could turn out to be longer."

"Yes, ma'am."

"I'm not exactly sure of the time frame for you to activate. We're still just looking for names. Could be next week, could be next month."

"Understood."

Other green-hand icons lit up and folks stated their specialty and what they felt they could do. The Lieutenant kept taking notes, letting each reservist know that they would get an email with their orders by tomorrow noon.

"Thanks all. Over and out. Have a great Navy day." And the Zoom call went black.

I clicked the little red 'leave' button and confirmed that I didn't want to stay connected.

The call to my boss, explaining that I was being activated was much longer.

"But...you aren't active duty anymore. It's not like you're National Guard." Rebecca sounded so confused. She was the Administrator at the hospital, not part of Human Resources.

Sighing, I started explaining again. "I'm in the reserves. It's in my HR record. It's why I have weekends every month when I can't work and then two weeks of duty in the summer."

"I'm going to deny it."

"You can't. You agreed to it when you hired me."

"You said two weeks. This is for a month."

"There's a pandemic. It's a national disaster."

"I thought the National Guard got called up for that."

"National Guard is the state, and Colorado has called them up. I'm Navy Reserve. This is Federal. And now I've been called up."

I didn't mention that I'd 'volunteered'. That would only complicate things more. Volunteering wasn't really an option; it was just a nice way of making sure you got a say in what you're going to be doing. I learned early to get my hand up first.

Six
Portsmouth

August 2020

For a Sunday morning before the sun came up, it was hot and humid.

The Navy Captain briefing us at Portsmouth was an ass and I wanted to give him a full bird. We were all tired; flying via C-9 was loud, bumpy, and uncomfortable. Landing at the Naval Station in Norfolk in the dead of night hadn't helped; we'd had to wait on the tarmac for an hour before the buses arrived to pick us up.

And now, this jerk felt the need to scream at us like we were seamen entering boot camp. Hell, I'd already spent almost two years at Portsmouth Naval before getting out. That was my first CONUS station after Gaeta.

I might know my way around better than this black shoe.

We were going to be staying at a hotel—okay, I don't care. There would be a bus every morning at 0600 to bring us to the hospital, where we would be given our duties for the day. Then it would take us back to the hotel, with a cold box dinner, at 1900.

I already knew all this; I'd gotten an info packet when I'd boarded at Peterson. I had read mine on the flight. I knew the drill. It wasn't that hard.

I had expected the days to be long, but I'd expected a little courtesy and understanding. Maybe I was expecting too much. There was a reason I'd decided to get out of the Navy instead of staying in to retire like my dad.

Or...maybe things were worse than I thought.

I didn't mind being in Portsmouth; Raven was in Norfolk—literally just across the river—and maybe I'd be able to see her, check in on what was happening with Brent, his other girlfriend, and the baby. Last time I'd called—to tell her I'd been activated and would be working in Norfolk—it had been hard to hear Raven's voice over the screeching child. I'm not sure she'd even heard me.

At least the hotel was close to the hospital, and the recalled reservists like me were the only ones in the building. I guess the Navy was renting out the whole thing. The room had a couple of boxes of N95 masks, bleach cleaner, and a large bottle of hand sanitizer waiting for me, with instructions on how I was responsible for cleaning my room myself, but that setting my towels and sheets outside the door would prompt clean ones to be left in a sealed plastic bag by the evening.

We wouldn't get to use all the amenities; we had to stay in our rooms when not at the hospital, hence the boxed dinner. We could use Uber to get something delivered if a restaurant was still open. Most were closed for eating in, but some had transitioned to pick up and delivery.

It was just after 1000, and though it was still morning, I was exhausted after no sleep and the asshat greeting; I would be going to the hospital in the morning. I should crawl in bed and sleep; I was almost falling over now.

But I wanted to call my parents, let them know I was here and safe, and then call Raven. I'd probably just text Gemma; last I'd heard she was still living in her old VW van, though I think the pandemic had put the kibosh on the traveling part. Dad would have told me if she was in trouble somewhere.

Dad answered. He was chipper; they must have skipped their online church service this morning. "Ho, ho, Anna. Safe in Portsmouth?"

"Yup." I settled back against the pillows of the bed. "The Captain that met us was a jerk."

He chuckled. "I think that's a requirement for advancement to rank."

"No church this morning?"

"Not for me. I'm in the living room, waiting for your phone call. Mum is reading this morning, so she's in the bedroom with the laptop all set up. I'll pop open the door and give her the okay sign once we hang up."

Ah, my mother takes church seriously. She'd probably signed up to read a month ago and wouldn't reschedule except for an emergency.

My parents understood how the military worked, having both spent their lives, so far, in service to it. Dad formally, as a Sailor, and my mom as a Sailor's wife. She'd usually served with the Ombudsman's office at whatever command my dad was at.

I yawned.

"Tired, eh?" Dad sighed. "I'm sure you didn't get to sleep on the flight." C-9s were not unfamiliar to him.

"Nope. Not a wink."

"I'll let you go then. Maybe you can call when you wake up and speak to your mother."

"Sounds good. Talk to you later, too?"

"Depends. We're still mowing the church lawn, and it's my turn to go over and drag out the riding mower."

"Okay. Well, be careful. Wear your mask. Use hand sanitizer."

"I will. You, too."

"Bye."

Talking to Dad was always quick and easy. Later, when I call back, Mom and I could go on for an hour or more.

I could talk to Raven for even longer, though. I texted Gemma's number first, just a short "Made it to Portsmouth", then punched in the number for Raven's cell. Rolling over, I hugged one of the pillows, propping the phone to my ear.

There was no answer.

I broke off the call and tried again. Had I touched the wrong icon? Called her work number instead of her cell? Had I accidentally tried calling Gemma?

I rechecked the app that was open on my phone and the contact opened; it was Raven's cell. I tapped the icon to call, and there was ringing, but again, she still didn't pick up.

I sent a text, letting her know I'd gotten in okay and the address of the hotel I was at, including the room number, just in case. We weren't in jail; she could probably come over if she had her car. We could meet outside, staying six feet apart, and talk.

Setting my phone on the side table, I plugged it in so it would charge, and took off my uniform shirt and trousers, leaving my t-shirt and panties on. I slipped off my bra from under the shirt and toed off my socks, setting everything on the other bed.

Laying down, I listened to the A/C unit rumbling under the window. The drapes were closed, but light crept in where they didn't quite meet.

Sleep was out of the question. Even though I wanted to collapse, I was too worried about Raven.

I didn't have a car, so I couldn't drive to see her. I didn't want to take an Uber—I'm supposed to semi-isolate. The CDC said I should isolate completely for fourteen days, but the need for help at the hospital was too great. There wasn't time. A negative test for COVID was making do.

I had tested negative back in Colorado—where they'd used the three-day test—and, again, here in Portsmouth, with the near-instant test.

But worry skipped around in my mind. Why hadn't Raven answered? I had told her I was coming to Portsmouth, and when, and why. When last we'd spoken, she'd insisted I call her when I arrived to let her know I was in and okay

That she wasn't answering was odd.

Unless her phone was dead and she couldn't answer.

My worry increased. In that moment, I really hated Brent.

Seven
Finally, a Call

August 2020

It wasn't until almost noon the next day—when I was in the midst of processing paperwork for incoming patients—that I got a reply text from Raven. Her phone had been dead because her charger hadn't been plugged in all the way and she hadn't realized it as she'd been busy taking care of Twila.

Stella, the baby's mother, wasn't well, though it didn't look like COVID. Her text mentioned calling me later, and I texted back, suggesting she make it a late call, after 1900, so I would be able to answer.

My cell trilled at 1901; I was just getting on the bus, damp box of unidentified cold dinner in hand. I answered, my voice muffled by my mask, relieved when it was Raven's voice on the other end of the line.

"You don't have to talk." Raven sounded winded. "I'm sure you're not even back at the hotel, yet."

I don't think my "uh-huh" was heard. The baby was crying. It sounded like it was next to Raven.

"Oh, God. Just a sec."

Raven shushed something—the baby— and I could hear a rustling of blankets. "Sorry. I've got the baby again."

She'd said I didn't have to talk, so I didn't. I was in an N95 mask, with a regular surgical mask taped down over that, and it was hard to breathe in the heat and humidity of the bus interior, let alone speak. My unit members were sitting spaced apart on the bus, one individual per every other seat, close to the windows.

No one on the bus spoke; most riders had their eyes closed, their heads wobbling with the rocking of the bus. It wasn't fancy transportation, just a school-bus style vehicle painted white with simple blue stripes and a Navy seal on the folding door.

"I don't know what to do about Brent. He ignores the baby and Stella most of the day. And she looks like the walking dead, losing weight, gray skin, lank hair. She's not coughing or anything, no fever; if anything, her temperature is too low."

I frowned. Those symptoms didn't spur a recollection of any immediate disease that I knew of, but I could look it up when I got to my room.

"It's like Brent doesn't even notice her wasting away. He's as fit as ever, so whatever it is, he hasn't got it." There was a pause. "I'm tired and all—the baby doesn't let me sleep—but I'm not gray and I'm eating fine."

Could it be depression? If the girl had been in love with Brent—I mean, he admitted it was his child, so they'd been having sex—and now he was ignoring her and had another woman...

"They spend time together, about an hour every evening, in his study, but I don't know what they do in there. I can't imagine she has enough energy for sex or even kissing."

Okay, maybe not depression.

The baby started crying again and Raven groaned. "I'm going to hang up; I think Twila is probably hungry and I need to take her down to the kitchen and heat up some formula for her. I don't want to take my phone with me. I want to leave it charging."

"Okay."

"Maybe you can call me later."

"Okay."

The call ended, the little red handset icon showing, and I could only hope Raven heard my agreement.

Eight
Regret

Late August 2020

When Raven and I talked a week later, she was distraught.

"She's not waking up!"

That woke me up and I sat up in my bed. "Who? The baby?"

"No," her voice dropped to a whisper, "not Twila. Her mom, Stella."

"Where is she?"

"On the sofa. She came out of Brent's office, like usual, earlier this evening and laid down on the sofa, with the TV on HBO, watching a movie, on low. Which is also usual." Raven kept her voice low and I couldn't help but wonder who she thought would overhear, especially if the girl wasn't waking up. "Twila woke up and I thought I'd take her to her mother, but she wasn't in her bedroom, so I gave Twila her bottle and settled her back down. Then, I came downstairs and she's still on the sofa, I thought just asleep, so I turned off the TV, but her breathing is funny and she looks waxy and I can't wake her up."

Oh shit! That did not sound good at all.

It sounded like death throes.

"Call an ambulance." I jumped from the bed, tripping on the coiled bedsheet, "and I'll be right there, as soon as I can."

"But-"

"There's no time, Raven. Hang up and call 911!" I didn't care that I yelled into the phone or that someone else might hear me and wake up.

I swore. Out loud, even though there was no one else in my room to hear it. If I had just bit the bullet, called an Uber, and went to see Raven...checked on this young girl who wasn't doing so well...put her in the Uber and brought her to the hospital—no matter what this "professor" said.

Scrambling, I grabbed clothes and a clean gaiter for my face, rushing so that I dropped the gaiter and put my t-shirt on backwards. I didn't bother to right it, just tugging the gaiter down over my head and strapping the N95 to the back of my head, scooping up my wallet to ram it into a pocket, then jamming my thumb onto the Uber app on my phone.

Of course, no one was available.

I ran down the stairs to the front desk, banging my hand on the little desk bell.

The hotel clerk looked like I'd woken them up, eyes bleary above their black face mask, but they didn't complain. They straightened their mask and cleared their throat.

"What's wrong?" They blinked at me, hand reaching for a phone.

"I need a car. Something to get me to a friend's house asap. I told them to call 911, but I'm not sure they're able to."

The clerk bypassed the phone and picked up a mobile radio. "I'll get our van driver for you." When someone responded to their call: "You're needed in the lobby with the van."

Then the clerk looked at me, their hand once again hovering over the phone. "Do you want me to call 911?"

"They live in Norfolk."

"Let me call 411, see if they can find out if your friend called 911 in Norfolk." The clerk made the call and spoke to whoever answered. "I need a little assistance—no, not police. Are you able to tell if someone called 911 in Norfolk? I have a guest with a friend who needs an ambulance, but they aren't sure if they could call."

I closed my eyes and bowed my head, praying for the first time since my gram's funeral in high school, taking in a long, deep breath, but it did nothing to calm me down.

The front lobby doors opened with a automated swish. "Hey, what's up?"

Turning, I opened my eyes. The man who'd spoken was tall, Black, deep-brown sleep-laden eyes peeking over his black gaiter; the edges of a black mask peeked over the top, the elastics wrapping around his ears and puling on them a bit. He wore a gray, short-sleeved shirt and black pants; the same uniform as the hotel clerk.

"She needs to get to Norfolk to check on a friend." The clerk was still on the phone. "Gladys is checking on any 911 calls in Norfolk for you. Go with Ron, I'll radio him when I know something."

"Thanks." I know my voice was too low, but my breath seemed to be in use somewhere else; I had none to use for speech. I staggered after Ron, who let me sit up front in the van with him. It was probably against the rules, but I appreciated the offer. I needed to see where we were going.

I gave him the address Raven gave me and we set off.

"Domestic?"

"No, someone there is dying."

Ron glanced over at me and the van swerved a little. "Dying?"

I nodded. "Pretty sure." He knew I had a medical background; the only folks staying at the hotel were reservist corpsman or other medical volunteers.

"And they aren't calling 911?"

Swallowing, I looked out the door window. "I'm not sure she can. Not sure she feels safe calling, if you know what I mean."

He didn't answer, but he did speed up and slide through a couple of stop signs and a yellow light.

The two-way radio crackled with static and he picked up the mic, clicking the button to talk. "Go ahead."

The clerk's voice was scratchy. "The only 911 call in Norfolk was 30 minutes ago, from Ocean View."

Ron glanced over at me again but spoke into the mic. "The address where we're going is near ODU."

"Be careful. Gladys can call Norfolk police to ask for a drive by. What's the address?"

He repeated to them the address I'd given.

The clerk ended the call and Ron set the mic back on the peg. "Sorry."

"Thanks."

"I'll go in with you."

I looked at him. He was older, his dark, curly hair touched by gray at the temples, but looked like he had been pretty fit at one time.

"I'm a retired Marine. I've seen some stuff." He paused. "I'm also a lay pastor in my church. Volunteer at a couple of nursing homes. I've seen other stuff, too."

Sighing, I tried to offer him a smile. "Thanks. I'd appreciate the company. I'm not sure what I'm going to find."

Nine
Death

The outside of the brick Tudor, two streets back from Hampton Boulevard, was dark. No light on the porch, the windows dim. Even the streetlight closest to it was out.

Wouldn't Raven turn a light on? I'd told her I was coming...hadn't I?

"Doesn't look promising." Ron set the van in park and cut the engine, his eyes above the gaiter roving over the exterior, pausing for a moment at each window.

The streetlight, two houses up, winked, not quite off and on, but dimming and brightening in an erratic near-pattern.

Ron stared at the lamp, his eyes wide in a face that looked a little pale, and pulled the keys from the ignition. "We goin' up?" He turned to me and nodded at the wide porch.

"Yup." I opened my door, stepped out, and closed it softly behind me. For some reason, I didn't want anyone in the house to know we were there.

The other van door closed just as quietly.

There was no movement in the street, which was expected seeing as we were in lockdown. I adjusted my gaiter higher over my nose, pinching the little metal bar sewn into the N95 mask beneath it, tightening it to my nose.

The street was quiet, not even the sound of an air conditioner's hum reaching my ears. It was night, and cooler, but it was muggy, like most summer nights here. There should have been bugs buzzing or frogs croaking; Norfolk had been built on bogs, and water ran everywhere, through backyards and greenways, all heading towards the Elizabeth River.

I could smell the rotting marsh grass.

We climbed the five brick steps to the porch side by side, though I stepped forward to the door and Ron stopped at the top step, craning his neck to see if he could see in either front window.

There was a window in the door, a sheer curtain hanging inside. I couldn't see past it.

Should I knock?

I pulled out my phone and texted Raven. Staring at the lit screen, waiting for a reply, I heard the slight purr of an engine and then a car door slam.

"What's up?" It was a police officer, wearing a black face mask, one hand resting on his holster.

Ron stepped down a couple of stairs to whisper his answer. "She's texting her friend."

"Not gonna knock?"

Ron shrugged and pointed to the unlit porch light.

The officer nodded and unsnapped his holster but didn't take out his pistol. "Another car is on the way, just in case. Also, an ambulance, running silent."

"Thanks." Ron turned back and he and the officer joined me in front of the door.

"She's not answering." I held up my phone, showing the screen with the three texts I'd sent, all with no response.

"Go ahead and ring the bell." The officer pointed to the lit button next to the doorknob. His hand tightened on his pistol.

I punched the brass button, listening for the trill of announcement on the other side.

There was no reaction from within the building.

Punching it again, I held it down.

Still nothing.

The officer leaned around me and pounded on the door.

Another police car pulled up and parked behind the one already here, but the driver didn't get out. The car's spotlight lit up the porch, the lamp bright enough to make me blind for a few moments.

A hushed voice called from above. "Anna?"

Blinking, I stepped back and trotted down the steps to look up, squinting to see beyond the light from the police car. "Raven?"

"Can you help us down?" Her whisper was raspy and she was breathing hard.

"Us?"

"I have Twila."

"Yup." I waved Ron and the officer towards me.

Ron came down the steps, but the officer remained at the door, peering into the window to the interior; he banged on the door again.

"Tell him to stop. He'll wake up Brent." Raven's words rushed out.

"Raven, why can't you come down and open the door?"

"She's still on the couch." Raven's face peeked over the edge of the flat porch, long black hair framing her pallor. "I've got Twila wrapped in a sheet. Can I lower her down?"

I held up my arms in answer, and a small bundle swathed in a cotton blanket was lowered down to me. I couldn't quite reach high enough, so Ron stepped over, his extra height giving him the needed reach.

"Got her."

"Who's that?" Raven's face appeared again.

"Ron. He's from the hotel."

"And there are cops?"

"Yes." I pointed to the one who was still at the door. "We need to get in and help Stella."

"I don't think you can. I think it's too late. I think...I think she's...she's dead." The words were punctuated by a muffled sob.

The ambulance pulled up, stopping in the middle of the street, straddling the spaces where the van and the first police car were parked. Two EMTs emerged from the vehicle, as did the second police officer from his squad car.

"Can you climb down?"

Ron had the baby in his arms, snuggling her, so I focused on Raven.

"I don't know. He kissed me." Raven's voice sounded faint.

"What?" I strained to see her face in the dim light. The spotlight was focused on the porch, so her face was shadowed. I was surprised it hadn't woken up Brent yet, or any of the neighbors.

"It's the kissing." Raven's hair hung over the edge like a curtain, like she was laying down with her cheek at the rim.

"Raven, what are you talking about?"

"He came out and said he'd kissed her too long." She sighed. "Then he kissed me."

Ron glanced up at Raven but moved toward the EMTs with the baby.

I nodded, keeping my focus on my best friend. She seemed...what? Crazy? Insane? Unfocused?

Delusional?

The second police officer joined the first on the porch and they spoke together in a whisper. I suspected they were planning to get into the house somehow to look for the body we were all pretty sure was inside.

Ten
The Mist

We'd finally attracted the attention of someone else: an old woman in a walker, wearing a thick, chenille robe, crossed the street to see what was going on.

"Someone die?" She nodded at the dark ambulance.

"No, ma'am. Not yet, anyway." One of the EMTs smiled at her; the other was checking over a sleepy Twila. "Just here for precaution."

The old woman looked over toward the porch and noticed Raven on its roof. "Is Miss Davis okay?"

The EMT glanced up at Raven. "She's talking, so we think she'll be fine."

The woman snorted. "Not in that house, she won't be."

That got the notice of one of the officers and he jogged down the steps to her. "What do you mean?"

"Oh, so now someone wants to listen to me." She clucked her tongue.

"Ma'am, please." The officer sighed and held out his hands, palms up. "I haven't spoken to you before. I would have listened."

The woman leaned forward; she didn't whisper. "Dark things happen in that house."

The officer on the porch groaned and shook his head. "Batty."

"I ain't batty." The woman spat on the ground, jabbing one finger at the front door. "That there professor does dark things. He used to be nice, smile when I said hello, but in the last year...women he dates gets sick, pale, weak, lose weight. Who knows? They might even die. But no one wants to listen to me."

I stared at the woman. She'd just described what Raven had been telling me about Stella.

"Ma'am," the EMT handed the woman a paper mask, "please put this on."

The woman batted it away. "I ain't scared of no COVID. Not with whatever that man does in there." She inclined her head toward the house to the right. "That woman in there might be able to tell you, but she's sick. He-" she jabbed a finger at the dark Tudor, "made her sick, too."

The EMT sighed and tucked the refused mask into a pocket. "Ma'am-"

"And those women, they let him make them sick. They kept coming back, getting paler and thinner and weaker all the while."

"Hey," I take two steps to the EMT, resting one hand on his arm, "that's exactly what Raven said was happening to Stella. That's why we're here. Raven called me about Stella."

The old woman stood resolute in her walker, chin up, her eyes sporting a hard glare of righteousness.

The EMT gaped. "But that sounds-"

The front door burst open, knocking the officer standing on the porch aside and through the railing to land in an overgrown azalea bush. His pistol, freed from its open holster, bounced over the lawn to skid on the sidewalk next to the other officer.

Pulling his weapon, the other officer pointed it at the open door. "Stop right there! Hands up!"

But there was nothing in the doorway to stop. A faint, interior light showed an empty doorway, a dark mist or smoke hovering near the floor.

Was something on fire?

Then...what looked like a pair of glowing yellow eyes opened in the expanding mass of smoke. It gathered, forming a dense cloud that blocked the light from within. It centered in the opening, a roiling black cloud. Trails of the darkness inched through the opening and onto the porch, tendrils seeming to feel their way along.

A rushing sound, like that of a flock of birds, reached my ears; like thousands of feathers brushing and flapping. But I saw no birds anywhere.

The eyes, intense, unblinking, stared out from the midst of the mass. I thought it looked at me, through me...into me. My insides grew cold, and the sound of rushing wings filled my ears; I thought I could feel them against my arms and face, scraping soft over my bare skin and I shuddered.

The old woman gasped and clutched at the EMT, her shriek echoing down the street.

Ron faced the threat, arms out, placing himself between it and the EMT that held Twila close to his chest.

The baby cooed.

Raven was silent atop the porch roof.

The mass undulated forward.

The officer with the gun took a shot—it sounded far away, far farther than the distance it was—then, a second blast, louder than the old woman's shriek, echoing longer in the silence.

With the sound of gale-force winds, the black mass rushed down the steps, tendrils reaching out to the officer with the gun, whose hand went slack at the touch.

It swept past me, and for the briefest moment, I felt a kiss; just the barest sip of breath stolen away. My lungs stopped, the air leaving my body, and an icy brush of...not fingers...tripped along my cheek.

Then, my chest tightened, my heart sped up. I forgot what was happening and stared into the writhing mass, my gaze meeting that of the golden glare within it.

And it was gone.

Eleven
Recovery?

Once we had Raven down from the roof—one of the officers climbed up to help ease her limp form over the side to Ron's waiting arms—the ambulance took her and Twila to Norfolk General.

One officer saw the old woman back to her house, calling her daughter to come pick her up. I didn't blame her for not wanting to stay in her own home.

There was a part of me that wished I was somewhere else, like on a C-9 heading back to Colorado.

But I wasn't. I was in the back of the other police car following the ambulance. Ron was headed back to the hotel.

The sun was just cresting the horizon, infusing the sky with a coral-pink haze, when we pulled up to the ER. The ambulance had pulled into the bay while we parked in the lot. The officer escorted me in; he wanted to make sure I was recognized as being with the two people brought in by ambulance.

From the waiting room, I called my LPO to let him know where I was and what had happened. I was grateful the police officer was still with me to corroborate my story. He excused me from duty for the day.

I was pale and shaky, so the triage nurse decided to check my vitals, too. The officer nodded at her and gently pushed me into the exam room and onto the gurney.

Another nurse poked her head in. "The baby is fine, just a little dehydrated. We're admitting her for observation. Your friend is a little worse for wear; also dehydrated and a little disoriented. We're admitting her, too, getting her on an IV and a sedative."

I nodded, but watched the nurse taking my vitals, or rather, the measurements the equipment gave her. My heart rate and blood pressure were still a little elevated, but other than that, I seemed to be fine.

She patted my hand. "You can go sit with your friend once we have her in a room, okay?"

"Thanks." I looked to the officer. "What about..." I swallowed, "Stella..." and took in a deep breath, "back at the house?"

Since we'd arrived at the hospital, he'd been on his radio, speaking into it in hushed tones, retreating into corners so as not to be overheard.

He cleared his throat. "Stinson called for backup and they checked out the house once the old lady's daughter came and got her." He sighed, glancing at the nurse. "They found the young woman on the sofa, dead, like your friend described. They found no one else in the house. No sign of this professor... Brent..." he waved a vague hand, "whatever he's called."

Closing my eyes, I sucked in a long breath through my nose. It brough the scent of chlorine and bleach with it. A familiar smell, but not comforting.

What did it mean? Where was Brent? Had he left the house and Raven not known? She'd been upstairs, in her bedroom, and then on the roof of the porch, obviously freaked out by the dead body in the living room.

The officer held out a card. "I need to leave now. I'm going over to help with clean up and securing the house for evidence collection. But call me tomorrow, I'll give you what info I can."

Taking the card, I stared at the name: Lt. Antonio Garcia. "Thanks."

He nodded. "You're welcome. Wish the outcome had been better."

I blinked. "It could have been worse."

He said nothing to that, just nodded a couple of times, then waved half-heartedly and moved to the door. He looked reluctant to go back to that house.

An orderly stuck his head through the open door. "Your friend is in a room. If you want to follow me."

I pocketed the card and complied with the orderly. We wound our way through the labyrinthine halls of the hospital, past several monitoring stations, avoiding some closed wards with big red warning squares on them.

"COVID wards." The orderly shrugged. "Sorry, we have to go around."

"I understand." I didn't mention that I was supporting the Naval Hospital.

Raven was asleep in the hospital bed, the monitor at the head beeping in a steady rhythm, her arm spread out along her side, an IV tapped into the vein.

The orderly patted my shoulder. "I'll get you one of the recliners and a blanket. You look like you should get some sleep, too."

He was back a few minutes later, pushing the promised recliner, a folded blanket on its seat, accompanied by a nurse with a glass of water and a pill pack. The nurse held up the items in my direction. "Only if you need them." She placed them on the cabinet that was set along the wall.

"Thanks."

I helped the orderly arrange the recliner near Raven's bed, but not where it would hinder the nurses when they came in, and got as comfortable as I could, pulling the warmed blanket up over me.

"Call if you need me." The nurse smiled from the door and dimmed the light, leaving the door open a slight crack.

Raven's even breathing was a beautiful sound, and I lay awake, listening to it for over an hour before finally falling asleep.

Twelve
It Still Comes

Raven and Twila were discharged the following day; Raven into my care and Twila into Child Protective Services. The social worker said they'd contacted Stella's parents, notified them of their daughter's death, and that Twila was safe.

That's all she could tell us.

The hotel sent the van to pick Raven and me up from the hospital. Ron wasn't driving; it was a young woman with short-cropped purple and pink hair. She checked my ID and let us in the van—in the back—and was silent the whole way back to the hotel, bopping along to whatever she was listening to on her ear pods.

Though I wasn't sure I was supposed to let anyone stay with me at the hotel, we didn't know where else Raven could go. She'd let her apartment go when she'd moved in with Brent, and all her stuff was in his house—and that was closed to everyone pending evidence collection.

From my hotel room, I called the police officer and left a message. I included my cell number, stating it twice, then made sure my cell was on and plugged in to charge.

Raven was already asleep on the second bed, fully clothed on top of the coverlet, her soft snores a reassuring reminder that she was alive.

I sat on my bed, ignoring the crumpled sheets and wrinkled blanket on the floor at the foot of it. How sick had Stella been? A part of me wished I'd been able to see the body, see for myself the emaciated, pale-skinned frame that Raven and the old woman had described.

The trill of my cell made me jump. I snatched it up, punching the green icon to accept the call.

"Hello?" I kept my voice low, but Raven hadn't even responded to the ringtone.

"Miss Johnson? This is Lieutenant Garcia, Norfolk Police."

"Good mo-" I glanced at the alarm clock, "-afternoon, Officer. This is Anna Johnson."

He sighed. "I hope you're feeling well. I'm happy to hear that your friend and that baby are okay."

"Me, too."

"I understand the baby is with social services?"

"Yes."

"And your friend?"

"She's here with me, at my hotel."

"Good, good." There was a pause and the rustle of papers. "So, here's what I can tell you: Dr. Brent Miller has been on sabbatical from ODU for the past year, living in Japan, researching and immersing himself in Shinto.

He's currently in quarantine in New York right now, has been since last week when all Americans were told to come home. I spoke with him this morning."

"Then who-?"

He didn't let me finish. "We've verified with his neighbors that they'd seen him around his house and just assumed he'd come back early. With everyone staying inside and isolating, no one really questioned what was going on at his house."

"But-"

"Is your friend available for questioning?"

I sighed. "She's asleep right now."

"Okay. I'm coming over to ask her some more questions, but you can wake her then. She's not under suspicion of doing anything wrong, we're just trying to figure out who's been masquerading as this guy and how that woman died."

"Okay." I stared at Raven. I remembered that black mist. "Lieutenant Garcia?"

"Hmm?"

"Do you remember that mist or smoke that came out of the house?"

There was silence on the line, and I knew he did.

"No, I don't remember any smoke or mist. Just the door bursting open and Stinson being flung off the porch. Probably the guy waiting inside—hit it with something hard—and then ran out the back while we were all reacting."

"Right. Okay." I didn't think I could admit to seeing a black mass of smoke coming at me, either. Even less likely that I'd say I felt it...touch...me. "Is the old woman okay?"

"She's with her daughter, going to see her doctor later this week."

They were going to make her out to be crazy. I felt bad for her. My gut told me she'd been telling the truth. Raven had been telling me the same thing.

"I'll probably be able to give you an overview of autopsy results when they get in. You know, just basics, to reassure you that it isn't some disease or something that your friend may have caught."

"Okay."

"But until then, I need you both to self-isolate. Probably not COVID, but who knows? I've contacted your Commander, so they know."

Shit.

The shift leader will be pissed and I'll get crap duty when I can get out of here and back to Portsmouth Naval. It was against regs to leave the hotel like I did. I'd be surprised if I didn't get a formal reprimand for it—even if my LPO had been understanding last night.

An hour later, when the officer arrived to talk to Raven, he made me sit in the hall, next to the hotel door, gaiter and mask over my nose and mouth. In less than 30 minutes, he came out and ushered me back into the room.

I sat on the edge of the bed; I'd thrown the sheets and blanket back on it, roughly squared, when he'd said he was going to come over.

"Initial pathology shows no signs of COVID or any other known communicable pathogen." The officer read from his phone screen. He slid his finger up; he was scanning a document. "Blood showed no sign of poison or other toxin."

Looking up at us, he shrugged. "You still need to self-isolate, at least until we get a full report." He glanced to Raven. "Although, you probably don't need to worry. If it was some disease that could be transmitted to others, you'd probably show signs of it by now." He stared at Raven.

Raven nodded. She was pale, with dark circles under her eyes, but didn't look like she'd lost weight since our vacation.

I was likely just as pale with those same dark circles.

"Oh," the officer raised a finger, like he'd forgotten something, "Stella Grant had a life insurance policy. A big one. Like half-a-million dollars big."

He waited.

I didn't have a clue why.

Raven just blinked at him.

He sighed. "You two are named as beneficiaries, along with her parents."

"What?" My voice was a squeak. Me? How would my name be on her insurance policy form? "I didn't even know her!"

"Look," he straightened, "I'm going to level with you: It's not just self-isolation. I need you both to stay here at the hotel, not leave town. Everything you hear on the cop shows. We don't think you two are involved. If anything, we think the two of you might be in danger. Whoever was pretending to be Professor Brent Miller was likely behind the insurance policy. We've got a call into the company for info. And my suspicions are that he's got a plan to get access to that money via one or both of you." He glanced at Raven.

I felt faint; Raven looked like she was ready to collapse.

"There will be an extra Portsmouth Police officer on patrol at the hotel until we find this guy. Both of you get some rest and I'll let you know if I find out anything more." And he tipped two fingers to his forehead and left.

Raven flopped back on the bed, staring up at the ceiling.

I stared at Raven. "What are you thinking?"

She took a moment before answering. "Who have I been living with?" Turning her face to look at me, cheek pressed into the blanket, she let out a long raspberry sigh before raising herself up on one arm. "I mean, I thought..." Swallowing, she closed her eyes and sighed. "I am one lucky bitch."

My chuckle was part gurgle. "Yeah, you are."

"Poor Stella. I...I hated her a bit, you know, when she first showed up."

"I know."

"And Twila. I did not like the baby being there."

"But you took care of her."

"Probably could have done better. Done more. Called a damn doctor."

"A doctor might not have been able to help. I mean...the pathology report shows there was nothing wrong with her."

Raven flopped her head in my direction. "Anna, she's dead. There's a lot wrong with her."

I couldn't help my snort. "I mean, they can't find anything that caused her death."

"Brent—or whoever he really was—caused her death. I know it." Raven turned her head away, setting her chin to her chest, staring at the bad abstract painting on the wall. "I just don't know how he did it."

Should I tell her about the black mist? The glowing yellow eyes? The word that sprang to mind now was demon, but they didn't exist. And they certainly didn't put insurance policies on their victims...did they?

"What do you remember about when we came to the house, just before we brought you down off the porch roof?"

She kept staring at the picture, but her eyes narrowed, her brow furrowing. "Not a lot. I'm not sure I was fully conscious."

"Earlier, when you were talking to me from the roof, after you lowered Twila down, you said something about a kiss."

"A kiss?" Raven tensed, the tendons in her neck visible under the thin, delicate skin.

"Yeah." I tried to keep my tone nonchalant, waving one hand in the air. "Something about Brent kissing her and that's how she died. That he couldn't stop...or... something like that."

"Huh." Raven relaxed but didn't look at me. "Maybe he'd come out before I went upstairs and tried CPR on her."

"If it was CPR, it wouldn't have been killing her."

"I was half delirious. I probably wasn't thinking straight and mixing up my words."

Raven stood up and stretched. "Okay if I take a shower?"

"Sure. Go ahead. There should be clean towels. If not, let me know and I'll call down to the front desk."

Thirteen
It s Here

The supervisor for my shift unit was not happy; I put my cell on speaker and let him rail at me from a distance.

Raven came out of the bathroom—there had been clean towels—and stared at me and then at my phone.

I shrugged. There was nothing to be done. He was pissed and I was screwed.

We almost missed the call from the front desk; though the Chief Petty Officer's voice was getting raspy, it was no less loud. Raven caught the flash of the light on the phone between the beds and gasped, pointing.

I muted my phone and she answered.

"Yes." Raven's voice was shaky. "Yes. Okay. Thank you." She hung up the phone and sat on the bed. "An officer is downstairs with my cell and some clothes and my purse with my ID."

I smirked at the towel she was wearing. "I'll go get it for you. You listen to Chief Wilson while I'm gone." I unmuted my phone. The stream of anger was still going strong.

"What do I say?"

"I don't think it matters. I haven't been able to get a word in since he started. I'll be quick." I grabbed a disposable face mask from the box left for Raven and headed down to the front desk.

It only took me ten minutes, white paper bag of items in hand, but when I got back, Raven was on the bed, lying in a stupor, Chief Wilson screaming "hello-hello?" on my cell.

"Raven!" I dropped the bag and shouted into the phone, "Gotta go, emergency!" With the call ended, I stabbed in the numbers for 911.

The center had barely answered when I asked for an ambulance, giving the name of the hotel and the street in Portsmouth.

The urgency in my voice evoked no questions and the dispatcher told me to stay on the line while help arrived. I did, but picked up the hotel phone to call the front desk.

When the clerk answered—it was that same one from that first night—I gave them my name and said that I needed them to call Lieutenant Garcia in Norfolk.

"Yes, ma'am."

I swear they must be prior military, even though they didn't look old enough to be out of high school.

"And I called for an ambulance. My friend passed out again. Can you direct them up here when they arrive?" The wail of a siren sounded in the distance, getting closer.

"Yes, ma'am. I hear them now." And the clerk hung up.

"Ma'am?" It was the dispatcher.

"Yeah?"

"You're in Portsmouth?"

"Yes—but the Norfolk Police are aware of my situation."

"There should be a Portsmouth officer on patrol right there."

"I know...but I really need Lieutenant Garcia".

The siren was outside and someone banged on the door.

I looked through the peephole, recognizing Ron, the van driver. An officer I didn't recognize was with him.

I opened the door. "Hey."

"What's going on?" The police officer tried to look around me.

"My friend collapsed."

The elevator dinged down the hall, and the quick-step of feet on thin carpet and the squeak of a gurney rushed our way.

Ron and the police officer stepped aside while the EMTs entered and started working on Raven.

"Thank you. The EMTs are here." I spoke into my cell and ended the 911 call.

It immediately trilled. It was the number for my shift supervisor. I ignored it and declined the call.

A breeze ruffled the drapes and I went to check the window. It was open, letting in too-warm air, so I shut it.

Turning back, the EMTs had Raven on the gurney, tucking a blanket around her and her towel, and were strapping her in. "We're taking her to Maryview. You need to come with us?"

I shook my head. "I need to wait for Lieutenant Garcia."

They nodded and rushed out, one EMT keeping his fingers to Raven's wrist.

"I'm here." The Norfolk officer spoke from just outside the door, standing aside for the EMTs to leave. "What happened?"

"Raven-"

"I saw" He entered the room, nodding to the Portsmouth officer. "Where were you?" The question was for me.

"An officer brought her stuff...clothes... cell phone...but she'd taken a shower and was in a towel. I went down to get it." I pointed to the white bag I'd dropped next to the door.

"So, she was alone up here?"

I nodded. "She was listening to my chief yell at me."

Everyone frowned at me.

"He isn't happy that I'm in isolation." I shrugged. "It's screwed up his work schedule."

My phone trilled again.

I went to decline the call but Lieutenant Garcia took the cell from me, answering with a curt "Hello, this is Lieutenant Antonio Garcia with Norfolk Police."

"Who?" It was shouted.

"Lieutenant Garcia, NPD. Who are you?"

"Chief Wilson, United States Navy. Put Petty Officer Johnson on."

"Sorry, I can't do that. I need to ask you a few questions."

"What? Do you know who this is?"

"I know who I am, and I need to ask you a few questions. Do you need me to call the PNH Commander? His number is on my speed dial."

There was a moment of silence on the phone. "What are your questions?"

"You were yelling at Miss Johnson?"

"Yes, I-"

"What do you remember hearing near the end of the call? Did you hear anything or were you just yelling?"

"Well...I..."

"Yes or no?"

"I heard someone talking...and stopped yelling. It didn't sound like Corpsman Johnson. It was another woman. Talking to Brett or something. No...no, she said he wasn't Brett."

"Brent? Did she say it wasn't Brent?"

"Maybe. There was static or something. Then the line cleared and I heard someone yelling for a Raven and something about an emergency then the line hung up."

I looked at Lieutenant Garcia and whispered in a rasp, my throat closing on the words. "The window was open."

He dropped my cell and rushed to the window. "It wasn't open when you left the room?"

"No. It was shut. I have the air on." I moved to stand next to him, and we both stared out at the near-empty parking lot below.

Fourteen
Home Safe?

I was sent back to Colorado after being told not to go anywhere else once I got there.

Raven was sent off to stay with her father, once she was again released from the hospital. She'd been in overnight, same diagnosis as before: exhaustion and dehydration. They'd hooked her up to an IV and let her sleep, and then said she was fine.

She may have been okay, medically speaking, though I doubted she was mentally okay. I knew I wasn't.

I had dreams of open windows with black mist creeping in. I'd wake up, shaking, sucking in great drags of breath like I'd been held underwater.

My windows were always closed; I nailed them shut.

Lieutenant Garcia called me every day, asking how I was and if anything odd had happened. He didn't ask outright, but I knew he meant had I seen any black mist or glowing eyes. I only told him that I was having nightmares, but otherwise, everything was normal.

Raven usually called about a half hour after I'd hang up from the Lieutenant. I figured that was because he then called her and they were done with their call. I never confirmed it, though, in case I was wrong.

She was happy to be at her dad's, even if it meant her mother ranting about playing favorites. She never mentioned being told not to go anywhere or about having nightmares.

I didn't offer that about me.

We just chit-chatted, talking about the plans for a cruise when the pandemic was over. Her dad had offered to pay for her to go and that she could pay him back once she was working again.

And though I thought about the insurance policy payout that might be coming—but really, would it?—I never spoke about it. Surely Stella's parents would contest it, right?—and I didn't mention that, either.

December 2020

"Miss Johnson?"

The call was from Lieutenant Garcia. I don't know why he didn't just call me by my first name. We'd talked so often, it felt like he should be able to.

"Yes?" I swiveled away from my work laptop so I could concentrate on the call. While it meant I wasn't distracted by work, I was now facing my bedroom window and the glorious majesty that was Pike's Peak.

The snow had crept down the mountain and flittered down from the clouds. Winter was cold and stark here in Colorado, but still beautiful. It was easy to appreciate that beauty when you didn't have to go out in the cold.

"This is my last phone call. We've wrapped up the case, as much as we can. You and Miss Davis are cleared. The insurance policy was bought by a gentleman fitting the description of Brent Miller, although we now know it was someone pretending to be him. And though we cannot determine how Stella Grant died, except that nothing showed in her autopsy so it was ruled natural causes, and suspect he had something to do with it, we can do nothing but clear the death record and allow the coroner to issue a certificate to the insurance company." The officer paused; it almost sounded like he'd been practicing that speech. "Just be careful; I don't know where this guy is or what he looks like now. He could be anywhere."

"Thank you for letting me know. And thank you for all that you've done for me, and for Raven, through all of this."

"That my job." And he hung up.

I assumed he'd call Raven next, and not thirty minutes later, in the midst of skimming through a very boring report of data regarding inpatient diagnoses that I had to turn into a written paragraph for a stakeholders annual briefing, Raven called me.

"Hi, Anna. You heard?"

"From Lieutenant Garcia? Yeah." I sighed. "Bit of a relief."

"Big bit. I was starting to worry that we were going to be found guilty of something." Raven's voice sounded freer than it had in months.

I laughed, but the sound was restrained. We were talking about death and dying and being held responsible for it. "How are things with your dad?"

"Good. He's been trying to teach me how to make gazpacho and I've not gotten any better than when I got here. I'm sick of eating it, too." She laughed, though it, too, sounded other than natural.

After a long pause, she mentioned the cruise plans. "You still think things are going to ease up?"

"We've elected a new government and they said they'll make it a priority to get vaccines out. I see the end of the tunnel." Hospital staff had gotten near-daily briefs about the vaccine situation. I knew that medical professionals would get first dibs, and that a few nurses from Memorial Hospital had participated in the Pfizer trials.

"So, we'll be able to go in the Spring?"

"Probably better to plan for the Summer, maybe early Fall. Just to make sure folks have been vaccinated." I'd get a priority vaccine, since I worked in a hospital setting, and of course that meant I'd be expected to go back into the office.

And Raven might get a military dependent vaccine, through her dad.

"I'm rethinking what I want to do for a job."

"Oh?" An email notice popped onto my laptop display and I wasn't really paying attention to what Raven was saying.

"I've decided to train to be an EMT."

That caught me up. "What? Why?"

There was silence for a moment on the phone. "I don't know. But in Norfolk, without those EMTs..." She sighed. "Even though they couldn't help Stella, they helped me...and Twila, I think. It must be a good feeling knowing you helped save someone like that."

As a former Navy Corpsman I wanted to laugh, but I held it in. "The hours are long and stressful. And think about how you would feel when you didn't save someone." I knew how that felt. It hit me sometimes at the hospital, running reports and doing the paperwork. Folks die in the hospital all the time.

I refused to think about those times folks died when I'd been on active duty.

"I suppose." Raven groaned. "I just feel like I wasn't doing anything to help with the pandemic, just sitting at home, absolutely gutted over a restaurant getting closed down. It feels... it feels wasteful."

That I could understand. I'd sat here for months, waiting for something to happen with Stella's death, wishing I was in Norfolk, doing something to move things forward.

I still wish I'd seen the body. I think— maybe—I would know more about what happened to her if I had.

What I think almost happened to Raven.

Fifteen

Gone

7 June 2021

On Monday, my alarm didn't wake me up. It couldn't; I wasn't asleep.

I just kept remembering—hearing—my mother's words from Saturday morning: Raven was dead.

I hadn't slept most of the weekend; rather, I spent two days in a fog, not really noticing anything, falling into bed well after dark to stare at the ceiling.

I didn't remember eating, but my kitchen sink was full of dirty dishes. It seems I ate, but I don't remember what.

I knew I'd drank. Empty bottles from Saturday night lined the back of the sink. I'd managed to finish an open bottle of Rosé I'd had in my fridge, then opened and finished a bottle of Merlot and Chianti.

There weren't any dirty wine glasses, so I'd probably just used regular ones, or drank it straight from the bottle.

Blinking in the middle of my kitchen, I stared at the coffee maker I couldn't remember how to start. There was coffee in the tin next to it, the ceramic scoop setting on top, but I felt like it was beyond my reach. Where were the filters?

Sighing, I turned back to the short hall and bath. Coffee wasn't going to be much help at waking me up. Maybe a shower would work a miracle.

It didn't. I dragged my weary bones out from under the cold blast of water feeling no more ready to take on the day. There was no way I was going to make it into work on time.

Rebecca, my boss, answered on the second ring of her desk phone. "Good morning, Anna. What's up?"

Her upbeat, cheery greeting was almost more than I could handle.

"Um...Beccs, I'm going to be late this morning."

"Oh?" There was a shuffle of papers. "Is everything okay?"

I paused. I was fine, but not okay. I wasn't sure I'd ever be okay again. What if...what if that...thing had found Raven?

It was a long time since I'd thought of whatever had killed Stella as a man. Even though Lieutenant Garcia had always called it a man, there was always a short pause, an unspoken acknowledgement that it was something else.

"Sorry. My best friend passed away on Friday and..." I took in a long, ragged breath. Why couldn't I say "died"? I worked in health care. We knew how to speak about death, learned all about the right words, that it was important to use them.

But right now, it wasn't the right word.

I wanted to use 'killed', but for all I knew, it had just been an accident. Surely, if it had been something else, Hank would have told my dad.

I now understood why family might be upset when we used those words—killed, died, dead.

It was final, hard, abrupt. It wasn't always as true a word as we wanted to believe it was.

"Oh, God, Anna. I'm so sorry." Rebecca's voice got clearer on the phone, but softer, hushed. "This the friend you were making plans with?"

"Yeah."

How many times had I shown Rebecca the website for the cruise line? How many times had Raven called me at work in the last month to talk about something she'd found out we could do on one of the island day trips?

The extra pay from those later Friday nights had been going toward the trip. Rebecca had been almost as excited about the planning as me and Raven.

"Anna, do you just want to stay home today? I can handle any changes that come from the Finance Officer about the report." Rebecca's voice startled me.

I'd forgotten I was on the phone. A part of me wanted to say yes, but I was aware enough to know it wouldn't help to stay home and cry. There was another bottle of wine under the cupboard; I'd probably just drink it.

"I...maybe..." Deep breath and I swayed on my feet. Did I want to spend another day like the last two? "No, I think I should come in. I haven't been outside since...Saturday morning, when my mother called to tell me."

I felt a bug crawling down my neck, and I swiped it away. It was just a wet trickle of water trickling down from my hair.

"Okay. Take your time, though. No rush for you to get in here. Use an Uber instead of driving yourself, okay?"

"Okay." I nodded and wet drops fell down my face. They were cool, not hot. So just from my hair.

They were followed by hotter, saltier ones, and I hung up the phone and went to wash my face and get dressed.

The Uber driver must have sensed my mood, because she was quiet on the quick trip through downtown and to the hospital administration building. She didn't even bug me about adding a tip in the app.

It was hot out, no surprise. It was always hot here in June; dry, too. Today, it was arid. I felt the heat; it engulfed me as soon as I stepped out of the back seat of the Uber, but I didn't FEEL it. It was just there.

Rebecca met me in the atrium with a coffee and a hug. "C'mon. Let's sit down here for a bit before heading into the office."

My boss was a little less than twenty years my senior. She'd been an administrator at a hospital in Boston, where she met her husband, a doctor, and they moved out here soon after they got married. Their first two kids were born one after the other, about a year apart, and the oldest is starting high school in the fall. The youngest was...extra.

Her dark hair was short and swept away and to one side of her face. Its neatness made me aware that I couldn't remember combing my own curly bob, and I ran a trembling hand through the strands.

"Oh, Anna." Rebecca set the two mugs of coffee—the hospital's emblem on the sides—on a side table in a dim corner of the atrium then returned to me and took my arm to lead me to an overstuffed chair. "Sit down, sweetie."

"Ahem." A clearing voice interrupted us. "Sorry, Mrs. Smith, but I'm afraid I'm lost."

Rebecca turned and smiled; I turned to see who it was but didn't smile.

"Ah, Dr. Curtis, good morning." She offered a cool smile and walked over to him, taking his elbow to spin him away from my tear-stained face and haggard appearance. "Let me get Candace to help you."

She was gone for about five minutes, returning at a bracing pace. "Sorry. He's the new hematologist. Bit needy if you ask me. Candace seems taken with him and should have no issues getting him over to oncology."

Candace was maybe all of twenty—so, young and pretty—and worked at the information kiosk. I suspected that Dr. Curtis wouldn't have an issue with her helping him, either.

My laugh held little humor.

Rebecca patted my hand. "Are you sure you're good to work today?"

I shrugged. Rebecca had asked me a couple of times about my relationship with Raven. In a lot of ways, we were almost too close, but in others, not. Not close enough for me, anyway. And Rebecca had picked up on that.

Raven never had. It wouldn't have mattered if she did. My feelings were decidedly one-sided.

I'd been looking forward to this cruise. It was like a prize at the end of a trial, an award for doing something good. I'd had plans. Plans I hadn't mentioned to anyone else, certainly not Raven. Memories I'd wanted to make; I felt like I wouldn't have a chance again. Not with COVID, not with whatever this thing was. Not with Raven living with Brent.

I'm not surprised that Rebecca had guessed.

"I'm not good enough to be at home. Not today."

Rebecca patted my hand, squeezing it just a little. "I getcha. Let's...let's just sit here and have our coffee. Hmm?" She handed me one of the mugs.

I took a sip. The coffee was strong, still warm, creamy and sweet, just the way I liked it. "Thank you."

"No problem, sweetie. Take your time, okay? We can just sit here, we don't have to talk."

There were times I took my boss for granted; this was not one of them. Tears trickled down my cheeks, and my sniffles were sometimes loud, but she just sat with me, not saying anything, wiping away a tear every so often and retrieving a box of tissues for me when my nose started to run.

Candace checked on us a couple of times, refilling our mugs of coffee when Rebecca asked, bringing a small tray of creamer and sugar so we didn't have to venture into the break room.

The young woman was a little flushed, and almost giddy. I guessed that Rebecca was right about her appreciating the opportunity to help Dr. Curtis.

"Anna?" Candace kept her voice low, like she was wary of frightening me.

I just raised a brow at her.

"I'm sorry about your friend." She gave me an awkward pat on the shoulder

"Thanks." I tried to smile, but it probably looked more like a grimace.

"Are you hungry?" She glanced to the clock on the far wall. "It's lunch time."

I didn't think I could manage going through the cafeteria line.

"Oh, hey," it must have shown on my face, "I can bring you something back. Even if all you want is dessert. It's Monday, so they have tiramisu."

Without my consent, my stomach rumbled. All three of us giggled, though mine was a little behind theirs. None of us sounded particularly happy.

"Yeah, lunch might be good. A sandwich would be good. Turkey."

Candace smiled. "So, your usual?"

I nodded. "Thanks."

"And the tiramisu?"

"Yes, please. That, too."

"You can bring me the same, Candace." Rebecca smiled at the girl.

"I'll be back as soon as I can." And Candace marched off.

Maybe I needed to give her a bit more credit than I had when Rebecca had hired her.

Sixteen
Mourning

8 June 2021

I decided to stay home on Tuesday. I wanted to call Hank, Raven's dad, and find out about any arrangements for a funeral or memorial service. I felt bad because I hadn't called him yet, only sending my condolences through my parents.

Working up my courage, I jumped when my phone rang first. Who was calling me this early? The number was not one I recognized, but it didn't include an 800 or 866, so I answered. I could always hang up.

"Good morning, I'm trying to get in touch with Anna Johnson." The voice on the other end was ultra-professional.

I went through my list of bills; had I forgotten to pay something? None came to mind. "This is she."

"My name is Susan Smith with Forrester's Law and Trust. First, I want to offer my condolences for the loss of your loved one. I know these times are hard and I will do my best to make this process as easy as possible. Can you verify that you are indeed Anna Johnson?"

"Um...no? I'm not giving you my social or anything." For all I knew, it was a scammer who'd made some type of connection between me and Raven, had seen her death notice, and was playing me for a fool. Our names had been in the Norfolk paper several times with regard to the investigation into Stella's death and had even made the national news once.

"Understandable. If I provide the address I have for you on file, can you verify it? I can then send you a form to fill out, sign, and send back to us."

"Form?" My stomach dropped to the floor.

"You are listed as a beneficiary in Raven Davis's will. I need to send you a form so we can start probate. I need to be certain your address has not changed from what was provided when she wrote and certified her will."

"Okay."

She rattled off my address and I confirmed it was correct.

"I'll get the form in the mail to you by COB today; you should receive it within the week, barring an issue with FEDEX."

"Okay." There was a moment of silence on the phone. "Thank you."

"You are welcome. And again, my sincerest condolences on your loss." And she hung up.

What the hell? Raven had made me a beneficiary? Shouldn't it be her dad? Or even her mom? Although, considering how Raven had felt about her mom sometimes, maybe that wasn't surprising.

And now, I needed to call Hank. What was I going to say? My rehearsed words were gone; I couldn't remember anything I'd planned.

I pulled up the contact list in phone and found his name: Davis, Hank. Raven's entry was just below his.

My heart ached looking at her name. I wanted to call and ask her what the heck she'd been thinking, making me a beneficiary. She'd snort before answering and calling me dumb to think she'd make it anyone else.

I tapped Hank's name and his number came up in my phone app, and I selected his home number and tapped the green call button.

He sounded tired when he picked up. "Hey, Anna."

I sobbed and gasped; I couldn't even say hello.

There was an answering sniff and throat clearing, and he stayed on the line, waiting for the rush of tears to subside.

"Shhh." His voice was soothing and helped the tears to stop. "It's okay, Anna. I know. I know. Hush now."

Did he know, though? "I..." I couldn't get another word out.

"I miss her, too." Hank sounded choked up, like he had also been crying.

"I wish..." But what did I wish? That she wasn't dead. That was a given. Was there anything else?

I wish I'd told her how I really felt.

That wasn't something I could tell her dad, though. That was something that would have to just stay with me, forever. Rebecca only suspected; I'd never actually confirmed anything to her.

"Me, too."

We stayed silent on the phone, just our ragged breathing letting the other know the line was still live.

"I haven't...um...arranged anything yet. Other than a cremation. That..." he sighed, "that was what she wanted."

So, there wasn't a body for me to say goodbye to. It didn't surprise me that Raven would have told her father she wanted to be cremated. Especially after what had happened in Norfolk. One of the first things I'd done when I got back to Colorado was write out a death plan and put it with my personal files.

"Her mother...well, her mother is..." He sighed again. "I don't know when Gayle will be available for a memorial service." His voice held a touch of anger.

Shit. That figured. That woman—I reminded myself that it was Raven's mother, and that maybe it was due to mourning, but...yeah. I didn't really believe that.

He sniffed. "Is there...is there anything you want at the service? A song, a poem, anything like that?"

I swallowed. There was but..."Not that I can think of right now."

"If there is, just let me know. And I'll make sure of your availability before we schedule the service."

"I'll be there whenever it is." Nothing would stop me from being there. Not even COVID.

"Yeah. Yeah." And then he was silent again.

I couldn't mention Raven's insurance policy. I wasn't even sure he knew about it. And what could I say? That Raven had put me as beneficiary?

And then it dawned on me that Hank probably already knew.

We were silent again, and I let my thoughts wander a bit. What else should I say? I found words popping out before I'd really thought them through. "How did she die?"

I wanted to know, but now was probably not the best time, not even a good time. I know I'd hate being asked that question this soon.

But this was Hank, and he just huffed. "Damned if I know. Doctors can't tell me anything. I just walked in to wake her up and she was gone. Laying on the bed, pale—I never realized how pale you could get when you died—but looking like she was asleep. She had a smile on her face, so I don't think it was a bad death, or anything. I don't think she'd have been smiling if she'd been in pain. I...eventually I closed the window and called for an ambulance."

What? He closed the window?

"Hank, why was the window open?" Maybe he'd opened it...please let him have opened it.

"I don't know. Maybe she got hot or just...I don't know. No one asked about the window."

Of course not. No one there would really know to ask about the window.

My sorrow eased, replaced with a slow burn of anger. Had that...thing...found Raven and taken her life, like it had Stella's? Why so quickly, though? Had it been afraid of being caught this time? Had Raven realized what was happening and tried to stop it?

But Hank had said she'd been smiling. Would she have been smiling if she'd been fighting?

Seventeen
Still Mourning

After spending the rest of Tuesday morning scrubbing my entire condo twice over—it was small, so it wasn't that hard—I decided I needed to try to find out some more information. I needed something to take my focus off my anger.

I was sure that thing had found Raven and killed her. And at a few minutes after noon, I realized that it might be able to find me, too.

I just didn't know why. Or how.

But that thing—that black mass of smoke with glowing eyes—was something I needed to find out about. I needed to make a plan. I needed to find it before it found me...if it hadn't found me already.

After a rushed lunch of microwaved leftovers, I got on the phone. There was no answer when I called the number for Lieutenant Garcia on the worn business card I dug out from the back of my wallet. I thought I might have gotten a number wrong—there was a digit half gone in a crease—so I tried with a different digit, but still got no answer.

When I finally got through to police information on a general number, I found that Lieutenant Garcia had died a little over a month ago. I didn't ask anything further, as that might have been taken as suspicious, and hung up.

But a search of articles published by the Virginian-Pilot turned up a small piece about his death. His wife had found him dead on the sofa one morning. It didn't mention anything about a window being open.

The only odd detail about his death was that it was eerily similar to a Portsmouth's man's passing. But he'd been older and retired from military service. There was a link to an article about that death.

Another click, and I found out that article was written about Ron Jarvis, a retired Marine who worked as a van driver for a hotel chain and volunteered as a youth pastor at his church. He'd died about a month before the Lieutenant.

Then I moved on to searching about sightings of black smoke. There was nothing recent, only bits of folklore that made little sense and wasn't really consistent with what I'd seen. How could no one have ever seen it before?

My inner skeptic laughed at me: anyone who'd seen it was dead. Stella, Lieutenant Garcia, Ron...and now Raven.

How many people had it killed? How long had it been around?

I stopped searching. There wasn't anything else I needed to know. That thing had killed them, and then moved on to Raven. I was the only target I knew of left. Unless that thing would go after its own child; a brief flash of worry for baby Twila made my fingers pause on the keyboard, but I had no last name to search for. And then, there was the old woman that lived on his street, but I didn't remember her first name, and I don't think I ever really heard her last name.

I huffed, frustrated. Why was it coming after us at all?

Because I'd seen it? Lieutenant Garcia had never mentioned the mist, hadn't even let me talk about what I'd seen. I'd never even asked Ron about it. Nor had he asked me.

Was it only playing the odds? Not willing to take the risk that we'd seen it? Seen it and would tell someone about it. It probably knew we had. We'd been right there.

But why would we tell anyone? This was the type of story that got a person locked in the looney bin. I remembered the old lady from the house across the street from the professor's home. No one had believed her, and she wasn't even talking about a black, shifting mist and glowing eyes. She'd only mentioned young women going to see him—it—and getting sick.

Surely someone would have checked on an illness?

That inner voice scoffed again. Why? Our government had let a raging virus wreak havoc in our country because it didn't want to admit we were vulnerable. Didn't want to risk losing money, risk our economy tanking.

Why would ODU or the City of Norfolk act any differently? Especially on a much smaller scale?

And if nothing was showing up in autopsies, what could they prove anyway? There was no way to come to a conclusion of foul play if there wasn't any evidence to suggest it.

That evening, at home in my condo, I double-checked every window, making sure the nails I'd hammered in were still tight.

Then I took a roll of toilet paper and stuffed the thin little sheets into the narrow, slotted cracks around the bottom and sides and top with a nail file. Maybe that would at least slow it down.

But I didn't know. If it was smoke, why did it need an open window? There had been drifting tendrils back in Norfolk. Then it had just faded into thin air.

Sleep eluded me. When I did drop off, it was to nightmares of Raven showing up outside my window, knocking, begging for me to let her in so she could get away from Brent.

I'd wake up, drenched in sweat, heart pounding in my chest. And I'd get up and check the window; there was never anything there.

Eighteen
Back at Work

I was early to work on Wednesday.

As soon as my alarm had started its chirp, I'd jumped out of bed. Sleep was not coming, had not come all night, and I had no reason to try to coax it anymore.

The office was quiet when I arrived, no one else at their desks. It was cool; the A/C had run all night, but the room would warm up a little once everyone was in and working.

My desk was in a corner, affording a little bit of privacy for the reports I ran. Rebecca's desk was large and had a six-foot tall false wall on one side, separating her from those who'd wander in the door.

Our receptionist worked flex, and we had an intern who filled in for the hours she wasn't in the office. We always had an intern. The one that we'd had before the pandemic had been hired in radiation full-time after we'd trained her.

We also had a medical coding clerk, but he was still working at home since his wife was an EMT and they had two kids under the age of five. It wasn't an issue; all he needed was a computer to do his job.

I settled my mask over my face—we were still wearing them in the office—and watched the clock. The information desk personnel checked in with us every day, and the first-shift employees would be arriving soon.

Candace was the first in. "Oh, hey Anna. How are you doing?" Her voice wasn't as cheery as usual, and she sounded a bit tired.

"Better." I looked hard at her face; there were gray circles under her eyes. "How about you?"

"Just a little tired. New man in my life." She giggled and sounded a little more like her normal self.

I thought about her reaction to escorting the new doctor to oncology on Monday. "You know we have a fraternization policy, right?"

She rounded on me from the desk where she was logging in for the day. "Of course, I know! I'm not stupid."

I remembered thinking I needed to give her more credit and smiled at her. "Sorry. I know you aren't stupid. I just thought..." I took in a breath, "You were all into Doctor...what was his last name? On Monday. You showed him to oncology."

"Dr. Curtis." Her chin went up and she keyed in her pin to the computer. "He's new. He's very nice. He's kind." She shot me a glaring side-eye.

"I said I was sorry." There was no reason for me to suspect she was seeing the new doctor. That would be pretty sudden, as it was only Wednesday, so...two days?

She huffed. "Apology accepted. I told him no when he asked me out."

Oh. "Good for you. And I'm sorry I thought you'd do something like that."

She laughed. "I met Sam last night, when I stopped to pick up something for dinner, and we ended up eating together at the restaurant instead of taking out. Then he asked me to go for a walk around downtown and I got in late last night." She shrugged.

I grinned at her, swinging around in my chair. Maybe this was the bit of distraction I needed to feel normal. "Tell me all about this Sam."

She spun to face me, and her cheeks glowed despite her pallor and dark under-eye circles. She looked happy, and for a moment, I was envious. I couldn't ever be that happy, even when Raven was alive.

By the time Rebecca arrived at nine, I knew all about Sam, what they'd eaten, and every less-than-juicy but romantic detail about their late evening walk.

He'd even asked if he could kiss her.

Candace waved and left for the information kiosk, taking a couple of boxes of disposable masks for guests.

Rebecca raised an eyebrow.

"New man."

"You?"

"No, Candace."

"I thought she had the hots for Dr. Curtis?" Rebecca poured a mug of coffee and sat on the corner of the reception desk.

I shrugged and spun back to my desk. "I guess all that changed when she met Sam."

"Sam?"

"The new man." I barked a half-laugh. "Maybe we should wait to talk until after you finish your first coffee."

Rebecca laughed. "The youngest isn't sleeping well; we suspect a cold, but aren't sure about taking him in to the pediatrician. Mike's still worried about COVID."

I'd almost forgotten about the virus; my focus had been centered so much on the thing that had taken Raven. "Well, it's still a valid threat. Especially when there's no vaccine for kids yet."

My computer dinged, letting me know it had finished compiling the data for a report, and I turned back to it to run the automatic format check.

"Yes, but if it's more than just a cold…" She let her words trail off.

I looked over at her. She was staring out the one window we had; it overlooked the small courtyard, awash in the colorful blooms and greenery of summer.

"Worried?"

"Probably nothing." Rebecca rose from her corner perch and took a long drag of coffee. "I think I'm tired of the virus and just want life to go back to normal."

Normal.

I thought about that word for a moment. When would my life get back to normal? The end of the pandemic wouldn't signal a return to the way things were, not for me. The 'way things were' had included Raven, and I didn't have her anymore.

It also included not knowing there was something out there that could kill and leave no trace.

"Do you believe there are things out there that we don't understand?" I watched Rebecca settle in behind her wide desk.

"You mean new viruses?" She looked at me, glancing to her screen so she could monitor what she typed for a passcode.

"I mean anything. And not necessarily new, but old stuff, hidden stuff we haven't found yet." I tapped the button to start analysis on the data so I could make the dashboard charts.

"I'm sure there are lots of diseases out there we don't understand everything about, or don't even know about. I mean, look at the ice caps. We're letting them melt and who knows what microbes are in them." Rebecca was squinting at her screen.

She wasn't interested in a conversation, and I'm not sure I was, either. How could I explain that I didn't mean a virus or a microbe, but some creature, being... thing...monster?...that was going around impersonating real people and committing murder?

The door opened and a white-coated figure entered, knocking on the door even though it was already open. "Good morning?"

Rebecca stood and walked around the false wall. "Good morning, Dr. Curtis. Lost again?"

"No, no. Not lost. But I felt bad that I'd interrupted something on Monday. I...I asked Candace yesterday, and she said the young woman wasn't in, but would be today. I wanted to offer my apology. I hadn't meant to make anything awkward."

Laughing, Rebecca waved a hand in my direction. "Well, Anna is in today. Anna," she turned to face me, "do you remember Dr. Curtis?"

"Of course." I stood and extended a hand.

He smiled—his eyes crinkled above his slightly loose N-95 mask—and took it, his fingers squeezing, perhaps a little tighter than I would have liked. Those fingers were cool, like he'd just come in from the cold.

Which I found odd. Because it was summer.

I shrugged off my misgivings. I was just being too sensitive. Seeing things where there was nothing to see. Letting my fears run rampant over everything.

He'd probably just had the A/C running extra cold in his car.

Nineteen
More Death

July 2021

There was an email waiting for all employees on Monday morning. I expected it to be about COVID, after all the numbers were rising again in unvaccinated populations, and Colorado had a large number of folks who'd not been vaccinated yet.

But...it wasn't about COVID.

We'd lost—well, the hospital had lost—fourteen patients over the weekend, most by mid-day on Sunday, and most from the cancer ward. Though it wasn't unexpected to lose cancer patients, we'd never lost that many before in such a short span of time.

Other than at the height of COVID, that is.

And of course, the email wound around to telling us to be wary of the virus, and though they didn't think the deaths were COVID related, they couldn't be certain until tests had been run.

I was just finishing the email when there was a knock on the office door and Dr. Curtis entered. He was a little flushed, his eyes sparkling in the fluorescent lights. "Good morning, Anna."

"Good morning, doctor." I turned in my chair to smile at him.

"Just winding down my weekend shift and thought I'd stop in to say bye."

He had taken a couple of steps in my direction when Rebecca walked in, two green and white coffee cups in hand.

"Good morning, Anna." She looked up from where she'd been carefully pushing the office door open with one hip. "...and good morning, Dr. Curtis." Her gaze darted to mine and she frowned.

"Just finishing my shift." Dr. Curtis turned to smile at Rebecca, but I thought it was a touch icy. "Dropped in to say bye and have a good day."

"Okay." Rebecca's returning smile was icy, too. "Bye."

He nodded and left, and I thought the look he shot me from the door was dark and that maybe...maybe that sparkle was just a bit...yellow?

"You know the rule about fraternization." Rebecca glared from where she stood with the coffees, holding one out to me.

I accepted the hot beverage and sighed. "I know. He came in here. You should know I'm not interested in him."

She sighed. "Right. I...yeah...I did forget. Sorry." Her shoulders sagged and she took a long sip of coffee. "The kid's still sick. We brought him in to the ER on Saturday."

"And?" I sipped my own coffee. Hot, sweet caramel. Yum! Rebecca could be the best boss ever.

"Just a bad cold. We have some medicine to run in the humidifier that should help clear his nasal passages and let him breathe better." She slumped into the chair behind her desk and logged into her computer.

I turned back to my desk to finish reading the all-personnel email.

There was a muffle shriek.

I spun around at Rebecca's outburst. "What?!"

"Fourteen people?" She was reading the email. "What the hell?" She leaned closer to her screen, her gaze sprinting over the words. "Was it COVID?"

"No." I stood and walked to her desk. "At least, they don't think so. The symptoms were off. And they were mostly on the cancer ward."

My brain jumped to a conclusion: Dr. Curtis was a hematologist, worked in oncology, and had been on duty this weekend. He'd been a little too cheery—in my humble opinion—for a doctor who had just lost so many patients.

Okay—so maybe they weren't his patients exactly...

Rebecca turned to stare at me, bright pink color tinging her cheeks. "And that man had the audacity to come in here and be cheery with his 'bye and have a good day'."

So, she too found his demeanor odd for a morning after so much death.

I thought about that glint of yellow in his eyes. Maybe there was more to the deaths.

"Beccs?"

"Yes, Anna?" She was leaning into her screen again.

"Do you think I could ask someone what the patients looked like before they died?"

She blinked at me. "Why would you want to do that?"

I sighed and looked away. How could I explain? Biting my lip, I worried it for a moment before clearing my throat. "I just...I have an idea of what might have happened, but I need to know what they looked like before they died."

Staring at me, she took in a long breath. "Anna..."

"I know," I cut over her words, knowing what she was going to say, "it's ridiculous, but please...please just help me find out this information."

She rolled her eyes but picked up her phone's handset. "Let me see what I can do. But don't get your hopes up."

It was probably just to humor me, because she was tired and frustrated about her son and didn't want to deal with me whining and sulking all day if she said no.

"Hey, Sonya. This is Rebecca in Admin. Are any of the nurses that worked the cancer ward this weekend still here?"

The voice on the other end was muffled, so I couldn't hear the response. I was probably too hopeful that anyone would be willing to tell me. Why would they?

"Okay, thanks." Rebecca hung up and turned to face me. "The nurse that worked Friday night is in this morning and is on her way down."

I could only stare at Rebecca. What would I say to the nurse?

I was still staring at Rebecca when someone knocked on the door. It was a nurse. He looked tired. "Hey." His wave was limp.

"Hey." I held up a hand, palm out. "Just answer."

He nodded.

"You worked Friday night?"

"Yes. Until 8 am, at shift change, but didn't get out of here until almost 11."

I winced. "Sorry."

He shrugged. "You wanted to know about the patients that died?"

Nodding, I held up my hand again. "Let me describe what I think they looked like, okay?"

He crossed his arms and nodded, cocking one hip to the side.

"Gray skinned, really dark circles, and frail, skeletal frames." As soon as I spoke, I knew how ridiculous I sounded. That was a description that could fit any cancer patient.

"Anna." Rebecca stood. "They were cancer patients."

I nodded. "I know, but-"

"That's exactly how they looked before they died," the nurse stared at me, and held up a finger when Rebecca went to speak, "but they looked very healthy on Friday when I came on shift. Most were not in the throes of horrid cancer treatments. They were all responding well, eating, drinking, even laughing." The nurse intensified his stare. "Then, when Dr. Curtis came in, that all changed."

Dr. Curtis. I swallowed the bile that rose to my throat.

"Dr. Curtis?" Rebecca's voice was faint.

"He was in with each of them privately. Said he wanted to talk to them about their cancer, yada-yada-yada—but when he came out of their rooms, they looked about dead already."

I dropped into my chair, almost missing the seat, and righting myself by grabbing the edge of my desk.

"Anna?" Rebecca stepped forward to set a hand on my shoulder.

The nurse stepped forward, too, dropping his arms to his sides. "Do you know what killed them?"

I looked up to the nurse, meeting his blue gaze. "Yes. Dr. Curtis...but I don't know exactly what Dr. Curtis is."

Twenty
Ending

The nurse glanced to Rebecca, who was staring at me with her mouth open a little. He glanced back to me. "Dr. Curtis?"

I nodded. I knew they would think I was crazy, but...I couldn't *not* tell them. Especially when Dr. Curtis had been in here with me this morning...alone...

Was he here for me? Had that thing killed Raven, and now come for me?

Swallowing the swelling lump in my throat, I groaned. "He's...I don't think he's human."

"Anna..." Rebecca stood up from her desk and took a slow step in my direction.

"...are you feeling okay?" She stretched a hand out toward my face. "Were you out in the heat yesterday?"

I leaned my face away from her outstretched fingers. "I'm not crazy. That...that thing...killed in Norfolk. First a young girl, then the cop who investigated her death, as well as the guy who took me to try to help Raven. They all died the same way."

"Maybe it was COVID?" The nurse raised a brow.

"Did those patients you cared for this weekend die from COVID?"

He opened his mouth to speak, then closed it, pursing his lips together. Finally, he shook his head.

Someone banged on the door and pushed it open. "Where's Candace?" It was one of the security guards.

"Isn't she out at the kiosk?" Rebecca looked relieved for the distraction.

"No. And I've gotten a couple of complaints already from visitors who don't know how to get in to see their family member."

"Is she scheduled for today?" I walk to the dry-erase schedule on the wall, scanning the names for today. Yes: Candace should have been here first thing.

Rebecca walked to her desk and picked up the phone handset, then checked for the number she needed to call before punching them into the pad.

I could hear the ringing on the other end. No answer.

"Maybe she's just on her way." Rebecca's voice was raspy.

"She always calls when she's going to be late." I may not always like Candace, but she's a reliable worker, responsible to the job and her coworkers.

The nurse looked unsure of himself. Like he thought he should leave but-

Another nurse appeared in the door. Her hair was falling out from the top knot on her head and she looked tired. She sighed. "Hey...I need someone to come down to emergency with me. I think the patient an ambulance just brought in is an employee."

Candace?

"I'll go." I tell Rebecca, already moving to the door.

The male nurse followed.

"Hey, Carl," the female nurse smiled at him, "I thought you were leaving?"

He shrugged. "I got a bad feeling about all those deaths over the weekend."

"And you were talking to Admin?" The woman shakes her head and scans her ID card at the doors leading into the hospital. "Masks. Sanitizer."

I hover my hands below the sanitizer station, rubbing them together the requisite 30 seconds, then pull a fresh mask out and put it over the mask already on my face, squeezing the little metal bar over my nose.

The ER nurse led us to a curtained cubicle, peeking around the edge of the drape before motioning us forward.

It was indeed Candace, lying gray-skinned on the gurney, dark circles etched below her eyes, her breathing ragged despite the oxygen feed to her nostrils.

I'd really hoped it had been a car accident.

But no. It looked like Dr. Curtis was helping himself to Candace. Or was it Sam, the new man?

Or...were Sam and Dr. Curtis the same being?

I mean, I should have guessed that this thing could take the shape of others. No one had suspected anything in Norfolk until the real ODU professor showed up. He'd looked and sounded just like the man.

Fuck. For all I knew, this male nurse—Carl—was that entity and I would be dead in one quick breath if he got me alone.

Hell, it could be the female nurse.

It could be anyone.

It could even be Rebecca.

I found my voice, or some of it at least, and whispered, "Will she be okay?"

The ER nurse shrugged. "We don't know what's wrong with her. Blood tests have come back normal. No infection. No sign of any virus, corona or otherwise. A neighbor called an ambulance when they found her apartment door open this morning and called in for her. She was found on the floor, nearly unconscious, just like this." The woman waved a hand at Candace's still form.

"Same as the patients this weekend." Carl licked his lips, setting his hands on his hips. "Keep a close eye on her. She may not have long left."

The ER nurse stared at him, then looked back to Candace, sighing. She reached out and tucked a stray wisp of hair behind Candace's ear. "She doesn't look like she's in pain, at least."

No, there was that. A slight smile curved her pale lips.

I cleared my throat. "I'll go let Becca know. We'll need to call her family and stuff."

The female nurse nodded and sniffed. "Yeah."

Carl took my elbow and led me away, glancing over his shoulder at the curtain obscuring Candace from our view before the automatic doors shut us off from the ER spaces. "That's horrible."

I nodded. What was I going to tell Rebecca? That Candace was in the ER, certainly, but what else? What would Rebecca tell Candace's parents?

"Real shame." Carl whispered directly into my ear. "It's okay. Let me help you." He laced an arm beneath mine and lifted, like he was helping me stay standing.

Looking into his face, I saw a faint glow of yellow in his eyes, heard the faint beating of wings and feathers in my ears.

"I know that was a shock, but everything will be fine." His mouth was close to mine, and I expected him to kiss me, but I was still wearing the masks.

He smiled, and his teeth might have been a little sharper than a human's or not teeth at all but a row of serrations in his mouth, just a row of sharp points, and I wondered if he was going to bite me.

Nostrils flaring, he breathed in deep, his nose long and beaked, and I felt the breath leave my lungs. My head swam and the world went gray.

He breathed in again, and I couldn't take in air to replenish what he was taking.

"Shhh." He stroked a hand down my head, smoothing back my hair. He must look like he was comforting me. "There's no place to run. No place to hide. Just give in."

He was right. I couldn't hide from him. There was nowhere for me to go that he couldn't follow—and I'd never know he was there, that it was him.

Closing my eyes, I let my breath out, lost to the roaring beat in my ears.

He chuckled and breathed in deeper.

And the world went black.

END

About the Author

Tara Moeller lives in the Hampton Roads area of Virginia, arriving there by way of the Navy. After serving six years, she left the service to take care of her only child and go back to school, while her husband was still a Sailor.

After graduating from Old Dominion University with a BA in English, she began working as an editor for DoD; she also acts as the main editor for our write collective. She has also contributed short stories to our anthologies (and anthologies from other publishers).

This is her fifth novella to be published by DreamPunk Press.

www.ingramcontent.com/pod-product-compliance
Lightning Source LLC
Chambersburg PA
CBHW071819190726
48292CB00005B/1519